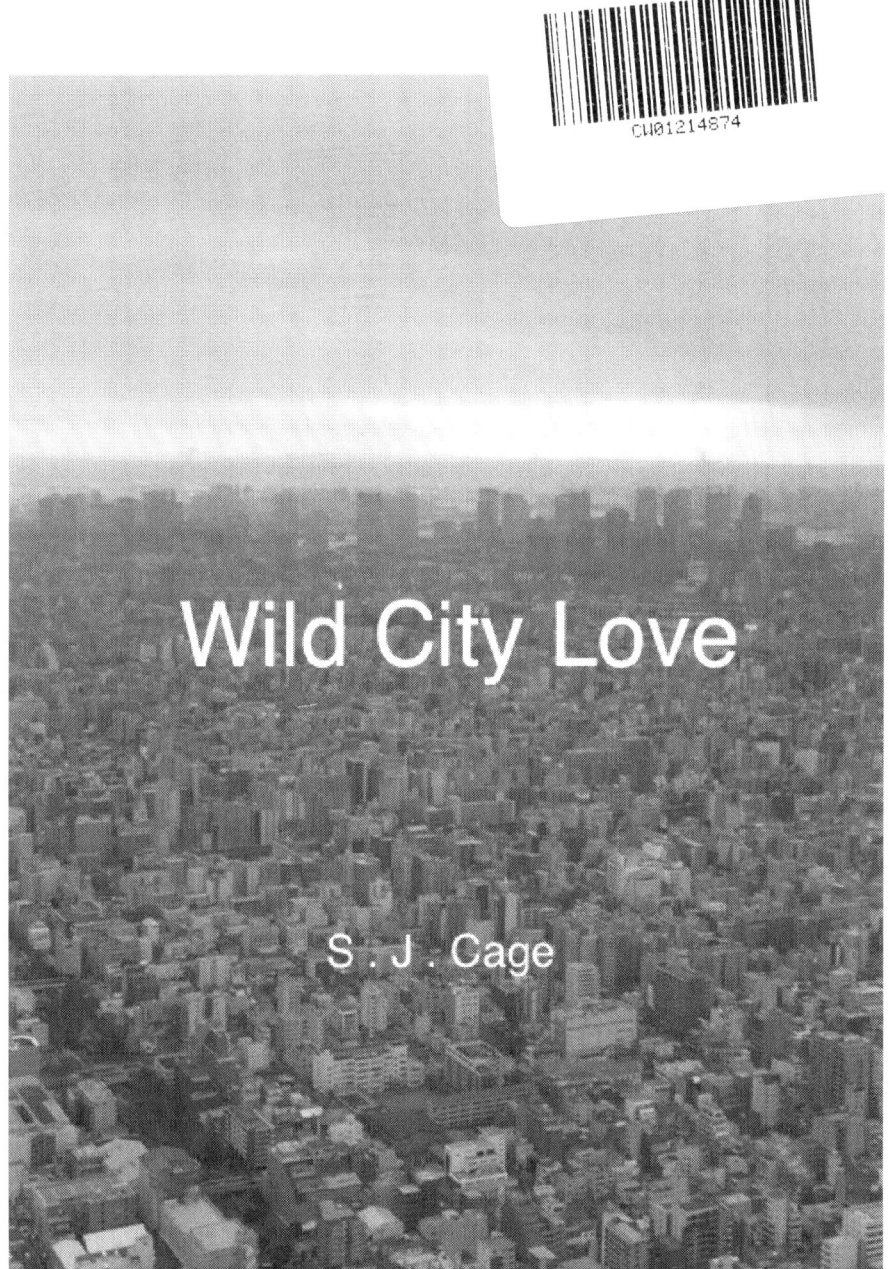

CONTENTS

Cover	1
CONTENTS	3
Lucy	5
The Dragon's Nest	21
Aladdin's	30
Steve's place	39
On the Run	46
Hokkaido	51
Hong Kong	59
The Prince Hotel	65
Rooftop Garden	76
The Albion	83
The Wedding	96
Paradise	104
Macau	108
Home	120
Police Station	129
Thailand	135
Back Home	145
NSW	154
Hometown	162
Tengoku	172
The Interview	184
New Chapter	190
Copyright	200

LUCY

It doesn't feel like only three years ago that I arrived in Tokyo, or nearly two years since I luckily bumped into Lucy. So much has happened in a short space of time and life hasn't always been a walk in the park. More like an adventure in a big theme park with bright lights, moments of madness and lots of people.

They say whatever you want can be found in Tokyo and after living there for a while I kind of agree. It might not be exactly what you want, nevertheless it will tick certain boxes. I remember my hunt for fish and chips, I found many different versions of my favourite dish from home, however they didn't tick all the boxes. Size was often the main issue with the absence of malt vinegar and beer batter. One good thing though - it's usually a healthier version in Japan with more than one colour on your plate.

When I first met Lucy, it was a beautiful clear day in Tokyo. One of those days you appreciate being alive. Breathing feels good, your energy levels are set just right and you feel you can do anything. I'd had an early start that morning, up at six, then I showered, dressed and had some cornflakes. After that, I spent some time in the mirror putting on my makeup and I was ready for the day. I don't use a lot of makeup and sometimes not at all.

Once finished with my makeup, I had a cup of strong coffee. I used to be addicted to coffee, drinking around eight cups a day. It was after I went camping and had withdrawals that I decided to quit coffee, however after a while I missed it. So these days I have about two or three cups a day and enjoy each one very much.

As I left the house I had a strong feeling that it was going to be a very special day. Autumn in Japan is often short; but very powerful and most Japanese people say it's their favourite season. You can see colours everywhere; especially outside the city. Autumn is also extra special because the heat and humidity have been replaced with cool breezes. Summer is very tough in Japan and the humidity sucks your energy. This year's summer unfortunately killed both young and old in Japan with it's extreme heat and humidity, not only Japan; many countries suffered with the heat. The summer was brutal and I hope it was a one off. Unfortunately, reality tells me I'm being too optimistic.

The autumn colours are sharp and varied, the maple tree is my favourite as the leaves change to a deep blood red standing out amongst the rest of nature. Another good thing about living in Tokyo is you can be surrounded by stunning nature within an hours commute. I highly recommend Oku-tama which is a small town in the mountains with abundant fun and nature. The Tama river starts there from a huge dam; it's waters are crystal clear and full of life. In the summer that is the place to be; swimming in the shallow river's cool water and cooking under the shade of trees on an open fire. In addition, there are the sounds and smells of the season.

One example in the cities and towns is the hot sweet potato truck known as 'Yaki-imo'. This is a small open back truck that slowly drives around playing a recorded voice singing about sweet potatoes. The potatoes are baking in a kind of oven on an open fire in the back of the truck. What surprised me the first time I saw it was the wood openly burning underneath the oven. When it comes you can smell both burning wood and baking sweet potatoes; which taste great. When you break them open you will find the sweet yellow potato waiting to be devoured. Another classic autumn smell in Japan is the ginkgo nuts tree, or as I call it the smelly nuts tree. They smell like vomit when freshly fallen, but that is only the outer skin. Inside is the nut that tastes delicious and they are actually poisonous if not cooked. You'll find them roasted on little sticks in the autumn. Their trees are also magnificent and the leaves have a bright yellow tinge this season as they slowly die and disappear forever.

Wild City Love

At that point in my life I was working as an English teacher in a conversation school. I got paid to help people learn and speak English through conversation. The lessons would start with warm up questions like,

"What do you do in your free time?"

"Have you ever been overseas?"

"What's been happening in your life recently?"

Then, you build a conversation and help the student to relax and enjoy speaking English. It's difficult for Japanese people to master English because the grammar is completely different and there aren't many chances to use English in Japan. Also, Japanese is spoken flatly; English however is like music. I always did my best to help my students and I think teaching is an honourable, challenging and fun job. As a teacher I believe we should always be willing to learn and try new ideas. A new teacher once asked me for some tips, and after some thought, I wrote down the following basic guide for him;

1: Note down feedback and any mistakes the student makes to be fixed later.

2: Aim for your student to speak more than you.

3: Don't use Japanese.

4: Make friends with the student and have a laugh together.

5: Speak at a speed that matches the student's level and speak clearly.

6: Have some material matching their level.

I feel, if you don't do number one then what are they paying for? Timing like most things is important too, don't cut the student off to fix a mistake as this can cause embarrassment and ruin their flow.

The second tip is because I've seen teachers do most of the talking. Typically, it involves the teacher talking for 90% of the class about themselves. The students don't get to practice their new language and they become bored or annoyed. This will also cause students to quit and the bosses don't like that.

The third tip surprises many people when they first start teaching a foreign language. If you make a rule of 'No Japanese', it will help students to try and only use English; there is always a way to communicate. It might involve interesting body language and gestures sometimes and you can also make it visual by using a paper and pen.

The fourth tip is important for good communication and that both of you enjoy the lesson. You have to be careful not to be too funny or the students will think you're crazy. A few laughs during the lesson are good and use of words can be very amusing. I have a few standard jokes that work. A student might ask me,

"Where were you born?" And I love to reply,

"In a hospital." Or when practicing ordering food they might ask,

"How would you like your steak?"

"On a plate." Is my usual reply.

The fifth tip is from personal experience. When I first started teaching, students didn't understand me sometimes. A kind colleague pulled me aside one day and told me to slow down, then we practiced speaking clearly in a mirror. He also asked if I was studying Japanese. I was and really enjoying the challenge. He then chatted away in Japanese to me and I was lost completely. He explained he'd thrown in some idioms and a couple of proverbs. From that day on my lessons improved. I do love proverbs and try to use them in classes sometimes or teach them. One of my favourites is, 'You only get out what you put in.'

The last tip is from being in a lesson and the conversation dried up. That's when it's handy to have some extra material and there is a lot of great material available. A news article can be used for an hour if done right.

To be honest, I loved teaching and as the proverb says 'What you put in is what you get out,' or 'The more you give or do, the more you receive or produce.' You see progress (usually) and it's interesting working with different people. I consider myself rational, optimistic and usually fun to be with. I think I'm a plain Jane; although when I dress up I often get compliments. I'm not very good at accepting compliments, I appreciate them, but often they make me feel awkward. I like giving compliments and watching people's different reactions. I think this world needs more compliment givers.

Many people say I look like Emma Watson (from Harry Potter) in her adulthood. We are about the same age (twenty six), height, build and we lookalike. I always reply with the same comment that I wish I had her pay check every month. That's the trouble with teaching in Japan; it doesn't pay so well and most teachers I know do extra work. I guess that's the same for most teachers in the world though, and maybe it's not such a bad thing. There's something to be said about needing your job, it creates great workers.

One of the advantages of living in a big city like Tokyo is there is always extra work. This can be anything from teaching private classes in your free time, bar or hostess work to translating jobs. There are many job sites with a huge variety of work. I tried hostess work once but it was abruptly stopped by Lucy. I believe she did me a favour by getting me out. The job involved dressing in skimpy clothes and having to look sexy. Arriving at nine in the evening and working until the last customer was finished.

The customers were nearly always sweet (but sweaty) successful businessmen who wanted to be pampered and do some pampering. We would pour their drinks, laugh at their stories and light their cigarettes. The clubs were usually dark, seedy and private and they are sometimes dangerous. The management are often Yakuza, (Japanese mafia) who are both respected and feared in Japan. They have a long fascinating history, but are a bitch to work for as a hostess. They always paid me well and made sure us girls were safe when in the club, but would turn a blind eye to some things. Also, if you ever upset them - you best disappear quickly or face the consequences.

On that beautiful autumn day, (my last night in that job) as I was leaving a booth, I bumped into Lucy. Both of us were tipsy and escaping unwanted customers. We collided head on and went down onto the dirty floor together. I got up first and apologised, then I grabbed her hands and helped her up. Luckily, she started laughing and that was the beginning of our friendship. Her laugh is contagious, loud, bold and beautiful. Actually, these four adjectives describe Lucy perfectly.

Once you've enjoyed her company; you want it again. She is loud, but lots of fun to be with. She is as bold as a crow, but also very thoughtful and caring. And, yes she is a beauty! Her beauty comes from good genes and of course her own looks too. Her father is Indian and her mother is British, both career models and still looking hot in their mid fifties. The first thing that made me dizzy looking at Lucy was her smile and her contagious laugh as I picked her up of the floor. After I'd picked her up we hugged each other tightly and it was a hug I will never forget. Her warmth and delicate scent made me even dizzier. For me, it was love at first sight, which was something I'd never experienced before that moment.

She pressed her sexy firm body against me and I could feel how perfect she was. Our hug turned into a long and deep kiss. I don't know how long it lasted but it was perfect. It was my first time to kiss a woman so strongly and I remember how good it felt. The chemistry between us was so intoxicating that I was lost for words after that kiss. Lucy however, managed a dazzling smile.

The moment was broken by one of the bosses who seemed both confused and annoyed. He looked ridiculous, not only in attitude, but his dress sense was comical. His over padded shoulders in his green and white checkered suit was a sight. Also, he was wearing way too much jewellery; it was everywhere, around his neck, on his hands and wrists, even in his mouth. His golden teeth though, made him look dangerous.

This was when I first saw Lucy's boldness. Goldy was looking up at us with his hands on his skinny hips and he hissed through his shiny mouth,

"What you fuckin doing bitch?" Then, mistakenly he grabbed Lucy's arm and went to take her away. She spun around like a wild cat and he lost his footing. He crumbled to the floor and there was a very audible thud as his head hit the table as he fell. I was stuck to the spot and not believing my eyes. Then Lucy kicked him in the head about three times and screamed,

"Fuck you!" We then ran quickly for the exit and met no resistance. Once outside the cool autumn air felt good and we kept running for about ten minutes.

Love at first sight does exist and that was my first taste of it. It's a feeling you can't control or create and I was in trouble from the start. Like an addict with their drugs; they lose control of their will power even common sense goes out of the window, except for me it was a drug called love. After leaving the club and getting away I felt scared, but loving being with such a beautiful wild woman. We got to an alley and this time I was courageous. I took the lead in the kissing and she didn't resist. In fact, she gave me everything and I wanted everything she had. My addiction peaked early and I was out of control. That was the strongest emotion for anyone I had ever felt. After the kissing and caressing, we looked at each other whilst holding each other by the shoulders until I said,

"Fuck those assholes! We are best out of there, can we go somewhere for a drink?" I remember those words so clearly, because it's unusual for me to swear out loud. Lucy smiled,

"That's a great idea and I know a good spot for this time of the morning." Then she grabbed me by the waist and laughed out loud. Her head went right back revealing her exotic neck. Once her laugh was finished, she looked me in the eyes and said,

"I don't know your name yet, but I know we are going to have some fun tonight!"

"I'm Katie and I'm ready for lots of fun with you baby." That was when I suddenly realised I'd left my handbag and my jacket in the club.

"Oh no! I haven't got anything. My phone, my money, my new Gucci bag and my jacket are all in the club!"

"Mine too, you know we can't go back Katie, that would be like signing our death warrants!" Then a look came across her face, a look that I came to understand as a sign of fun, craziness and trouble all blended together. A naughty smile appeard on her beautiful face.

"Don't worry, I'll get Tracey to get our stuff when she leaves the club and by the way I'm Lucy." Then she kissed me on the lips and arm in arm led the way to, "The

Dragon's Nest."

THE DRAGON'S NEST

The Dragon's Nest is an infamous basement club that is open to everybody, also, it has no cover charge which was unusual in that area. The area is famous for hostess clubs, nightclubs, strip clubs, fetish clubs, expensive restaurants and dodgy massage parlours. It's probably the most international area in Tokyo, the clientele is a mix of all walks of life and sometimes you'll see famous people there. Mainly, it's expats looking for a good time, locals who like to party and lots of military. In the day it smells like it looks, abused, rundown and rotting, but at night it can feel magical. It's called 'Roppongi' and is one long street full to the brim with adult only entertainment. It's one of the most dangerous places in Japan and every night of the week something's happening.

The Dragon's Nest is a classic with free

entry and cheap watered down booze. It's also well known as a drug den and at two in the morning on a Thursday night it was lively. As we walked into the club through the big wooden door, the darkness surrounded us which was a big contrast to the bright street. There were some young, well dressed caucasian men, noisily playing pool in the corner and they stopped playing to stare at us. You could see what they wanted from a mile. They were American military, cashed up, horny as hell with no inhibitions. Most people don't mess with them because they could be dangerous when pushed.

There was a corner booth with a big fat western businessman entertaining three pretty European looking ladies. They were having fun with sugar daddy. This was a common sight and as they say, 'money talks'. On their table was champagne chilling in buckets and the booth was full of false laughter.

The bar was busy, however Lucy managed to find a space. I could see she knew the barman and he was looking at her longingly. He was a big guy and probably the clubs security too. He was dressed all in denim, unshaven and he looked like a ladies man to me. I remember feeling jealous as they stood their chatting and smiling at each other. It all looked way too friendly for my liking. That's when I saw the man pass her a large roll of cash. She quickly slipped it in her top, turned and winked at me.

I didn't want to be in a bar so close to the club. I was nervous and the shadows all around kept moving. I didn't know much about the Yakuza, but I knew they ran the underworld in Japan. The stories I'd heard ranged from murder, to helping people after natural disasters with aid and distributing food, but I didn't think they would want to play Robin Hood with us though. Suddenly, I was pulled out of my thoughts by Lucy's kiss on my neck and her words.

"You look worried, it's going to be okay Katie, don't worry! My friend Steve is sending a message to Tracey right now." Then Steve came over,

"I sent a message for you and I'll let you darlings know when she gets back to me." Steve was good looking and obviously a Londoner from his accent. He looked very comfortable in his skin with a mix of danger and kindness. I saw both in his eyes, or was it lust? Then he asked what I wanted to drink.

"You must be a mind reader. Can I have a gin and tonic please?" Then Lucy joined in,

"Make that a double Steve. And I'll have the same."

"All right my darlings, I bet you both love a large one don't you!" He brought our drinks over and we went into the shadows. Luckily, we found a table and sat down. We touched glasses and Lucy made a toast.

"To me and you and whatever comes next." Then she downed her drink in one, licked her lips and smiled that killer smile at me. I told her I wasn't comfortable staying so close to the club. She agreed, and we decided to get a taxi out of town to find a hotel. I reminded her that I didn't have any money and she revealed the cash down her top. Without realising, she also showed me the shape of her perk breasts and I was horny again within seconds. She told me we could pick up our stuff tomorrow from Steve's place, then Lucy left me for a minute and went over to talk with Steve again. While she was at the bar one of the military guys came over and sat in her seat,

"Hello beautiful. Can I buy you a drink? I'm Carl and you are…?"

"In love with that lady over there."

"Oh, lesbians, awesome, can I watch?" I couldn't believe he said that.

"Only if you let us watch you and your friends first!"

"You don't know what your missing little lady!" Then he stood up knocking over his seat and left me alone. Isn't it funny how sometimes in the busiest of places you can feel the most lonely. That was how I felt, so I got up and went to Lucy.

She was speaking to Steve and when he saw me he gave a thumbs up from behind the bar.

"Lucy, I don't feel comfortable in here. Can we leave like now?"

"Everything is set Katie. Let's go have a private party together." Just as we were leaving, a man stepped out of the shadows and blocked our exit.

"Leaving so soon ladies?" He slurred, obviously drunk. Straightaway, I didn't like him. You know that feeling in your gut when you know something is wrong. He looked like a typical Yakuza and even had a big scar across one eye. Yakuza or not he was trouble.

"I know you." He said looking at Lucy. Next, he spread his arms open and offered to buy us both drinks. I didn't know what to say, he looked dangerous. Lucy was quick again,

"Sorry handsome, we definitely don't

know you and our husbands are waiting outside for us!" We went around him, through the door and back onto the street.

It was good to be outside again, yet at the same time scary. I felt danger all around us and there were all kinds of people around. Everywhere you looked something was happening. We walked to the main crossing and witnessed a fight between two Japanese men right in front of us. It happened in slow motion as the bigger of the two men grabbed the others shirt with two hands. Next, he pushed and they both went down. The bigger man had the advantage for a moment until the smaller guy twisted and landed on top. He got about three good head punches in before he was pulled off. Lucy, pulled me in the opposite direction and flagged down a taxi.

Once inside the taxi I was relieved and confident we could escape. We looked at each other and kissed. Wow, what a wild and invigorating kisser she was. The taxi driver was trying to get our attention and that made us both laugh.

"Where shall we go?"

"Let's get out of town and find a love hotel Katie." So Lucy said to the driver.

"Please take us to a love hotel out of town." The taxi driver smiled a knowing smile,

"You want to go Aladdin's. Good hotel. It's thirty minutes from here and cost about five thousand yen, (about fifty US dollars).

"Perfect." was Lucy's reply.

The taxi drive was comforting and we talked constantly feeling safe together. We found out that we had both only been working in the club for a month, so that was why we didn't know each other. I had seen her but that was all, in the clubs you're paid to talk to customers not other staff. I could feel the chemistry constantly between us, plus there was instant friendship. We both agreed it was a good idea to escape the club. There are many horror stories about things going wrong for the girls, sadly, sometimes death.

We made out a little in the taxi during the ride, fondling and teasing each other. Biting and caressing and testing boundaries. Her body was driving me crazy, so firm and shapely and I felt like I was in a wonderful dream. By the time we reached the hotel, I was like a cat on heat. She paid the taxi driver and the doors automatically opened for us, well with the driver pushing a button on his panel.

As soon as I got out of the taxi, I knew it was a love hotel, you can see them from a mile off.

ALADDIN'S

Love hotels are everywhere in Japan and they are popular with all walks of life. From couples looking for a place to make love, adulterous couples looking for privacy, or people looking for a cheap and interesting place to stay. Aladdin's was a typical Japanese love hotel and easy to find with it's flashing neon lights.

When you walk in through a private entrance you are greeted by a faceless receptionist behind a one way vision screen with a slot to speak through. This is also used for payment and collecting keys. You choose how long you want and that one had a minimum stay of ninety minutes for about fifty US dollars, or a long stay which Lucy chose of nine hours for one hundred dollars. Then you are passed a key and off you go.

After the elevator ride and the long corridor we found our room. The corridor smelt strange, I think it was scented air freshener which wasn't working properly. There were also different sounds coming through the doors which made us laugh. The room was purpose built for love making with a huge waterbed taking centre stage. It was glowing from the lamps and had a mirror directly above on the ceiling. There was a shower room with a Jacuzzi that looked very inviting! There was a mini bar that was well stocked with bottles of drinks and snacks, (at extra cost), and all sorts of oils with a box of condoms were by the bed, free of charge.

Lucy didn't waste time as she started moving to the music coming from somewhere and stripped slowly. First the dress which she took off slowly and close up. I couldn't resist looking at her in the mirrors which were everywhere. Next, was her bra and the money fell on the floor. She didn't even notice the money and I didn't care about it either. She asked me to remove her G-string but made it difficult. Each time I got my hands on her panties she pulled away from me. I ended up chasing her around the room which made me wild. It was a new sensation for me and I loved it, the more she teased me, the wilder I got. She too looked wild and a little dangerous in a very sexy way. God! What a body she had. Her skin was a beautiful colour, tanned all over and silky. She looked similar to Pocahontas. In fact, I had the feeling I was in a Disney movie made for me. How did this happen to me? Me... a shy Australian girl now with this beautiful Asian Goddess. She continued dancing for a while and doing different positions in various places in the room. She caught me watching her in the ceiling mirror and spoke for the second time in that room.

"Come on Katie, don't be shy, it's your turn now!" I think I was too slow for her liking because the next thing that happened was her grabbing me and pushing me onto the bed. Before I knew it I was naked. She was being rough and hurting me a little. She was biting and scratching me with what seemed like desperation. I tried escaping and did a few times, however this made her wilder and stronger and

I succumbed to her power after a while. She took control and it wasn't long before I was shaking and groaning with pleasure.

She seemed to know exactly what I needed and it was the first time in my life to be devoured like that. There was no hesitation, no holding back, no worries…just pleasure. My orgasm was like never before making me convulse and drawing blood from biting my bottom lip. Then it was my turn, I teased her with my tongue and body and I pushed away and danced for her. I made her chase me then catch me. We were sweating and very noisy until she returned the compliment of shuddering in pleasure.

I remember feeling flushed, happy and wanting no more than to stay in that position together forever with our bodies feeling a perfect match. We were out of breath for a while and that moment of satisfaction is **a rare and wonderful feeling.**

After sometime we made our way to the Jacuzzi. What a treat after everything that had happened that night. I think it's one of the best ways to relax and release stress.

We washed each other slowly, paying attention to every part of the body and I think we spent about an hour in that tub! When we were finally finished it was towel time. We dried each other and then we started talking.

"That was incredible and you are amazing Lucy!"

"I know Katie." This made us roll around on the bed in laughter for ages.

"You realise we have to be very careful where we go now Katie. In fact, we won't be safe in Tokyo anymore, I'm sure about that." That changed the mood quickly. The power of words, I went from heaven to hell in seconds.

"Yes we do, I feel we have to get far away to be safe, somewhere they can't find us, will you leave with me? We could go on the run together." I said this slowly and thoughtfully realising my simple life had just been turned upside down. The club owners knew enough to find us in Tokyo, but that was all. 'Love conquers all' they say and this was going to be the first time to put that to the test for me. I looked at Lucy and again had that strong feeling of love. I knew that I'd do anything to be with her. It also seemed mutual and that made my feelings even stronger. She'd gone from a wild animal to an insecure human; looking at me for reassurance that everything would be okay. After thinking for a while I had a crazy idea.

"How about going far away and getting new jobs? We could go to Hokkaido. It's the most northern part of Japan and no one will find us there." She looked at me deep in thought and nodded her head slowly in agreement.

"Okay, let's get our stuff tomorrow, pack and catch the Shinkansen, this is mad, but it can work, we can work Katie. It sounds completely crazy I know, but these are my feelings and I've never felt this way before about anyone. It feels so right. Let's get some sleep now and get an early start."

We didn't sleep much though and made love again, although much more gently and lovingly. It was even better that way than the first time for me.

I should've been shattered but my mind was doing overtime with thoughts of gang beatings, thugs chasing me down streets and around tables. I saw all the faces from that crazy night so clearly and very real; even the places were realistic. It was so real I wasn't sure where I was. Then I'd find myself squeezing Lucy in her sleep. Lucy slept like a log and she looked beautiful in her sleep. I must of got some sleep because I remember being woken up by the smell of coffee and Lucy playing with my hair.

"Come on sleepy head, how about making love again, then going to Steve's place. He should have our stuff by now hopefully, here drink this coffee." She fed me the coffee like a baby and it tasted like nectar. Then she made love to me. Not gently like I expected, but more like it was our last time together. Afterwards, the room was a mess and we made an effort to clean it up a little. We were a mess too and in need of a change of clothes. We took a shower together and I started feeling human again, then we called a taxi from the room which came within ten minutes. It was my first time to see a clock that day in the car. It was eleven in the morning and a beautiful autumn day. We kept our thoughts to ourselves in the taxi and enjoyed the ride. Everything was flashing past and looking normal, however I didn't feel normal at all.

I couldn't think straight, so gave up on that and decided to relax into Lucy's arms. Tokyo is a great city, and to see it by car is recommended. One minute your surrounded by buildings both old and ultra modern, then the next your surrounded by big blocks of apartments and factories. It's always an overload of the senses and there are so many people going about their business. It was like watching a slow movie and I was a little sad about leaving Tokyo as I had grown very attached to it. So different to my hometown back in Australia.

"Where did you grow up Lucy?"

"By the seaside in a small English town

when I was little and I loved it there. Then, from the age of about six we moved a lot because of my parent's work. From the age of six to sixteen we had moved ten times. I went to six different schools and was always the new girl, unfortunately, I always mixed with the wrong crowd. Mind you, I wouldn't change it, life was never dull and I've got friends everywhere. **I can also adapt easily to new situations, people and places."**

STEVE'S PLACE

We became quiet for the last part of the ride, comfortable holding each other. Sometimes, there is no need for conversation with someone special and that was one of those moments. I had a few flashbacks of the night before and each one filled me with dread. Did that all really happen or was it just a dream. Unfortunately, I knew it wasn't a dream. From this day on we were in danger. I thought about what I had said last night about going to Hokkaido. Was it a good idea? Would we be safe there? Then I thought about the time and reality punched me in the face.

"Oh my god Lucy, I should be at work by now, they're gonna be mad!" I'd never missed a day without it being pre-planned and there would be students waiting for their teacher. My phone must be ringing like mad. Lucy laughed and looked at me with surprise.

"Your work is definately the least of our worries babe. They won't kill you, but the boys from the club might, let's call later and…umm… give some excuse."

"What can I tell them?"

"How about just saying a private emergency came up and you need to go back home indefinitely."

"I can't think of anything better, they say honesty is the best policy, but not today." Lucy stopped the taxi and paid him. She took the money from her roll of notes and put it back in her top. I'd forgotten about the money and the amount surprised me.

Steve's place consisted of a room that had just enough space for a bed, a wardrobe and a suitcase. The entrance hall was just big enough for the kitchen sink, a few cabinets and a portable double ring gas cooker. You had to walk through brushing the sides before you entered the shoebox bedroom.

There was also a door to the plastic lined bathroom that served as a shower room and toilet all in one. These are standard living quarters in big Japanese cities with little balconies.

Steve was there in bed with Tracey and the room smelled of sex and sweat. It's a distinctive smell and by the looks on their faces they hadn't had much sleep. There was drug paraphernalia on the suitcase that was being used as a makeshift table. I could see weed, a bag of white powder and a mirror with traces of powder on it. Tracey broke the ice by getting out of bed and making small lines of powder for everyone. Without speaking they all did a line. I was last and Lucy passed me the rolled up note,

"This will make the day better babe. Trust me, it's only coke."

"Only coke, I've never done it before"

"Come on Katie, don't be a kill joy!" Steve pushed the suitcase towards me as he said this and I saw the anger in his eyes again,

I sniffed it up and sat back. It didn't take long to start having an effect, I felt both edgy and relaxed at the same time. I couldn't believe what I'd just done, but it felt right at that moment. Within a short time I lost all concept of time and what was important. Our conversations were about nothing and everything. We all talked and laughed together. We put some music on and drank some cold beers. We talked about last night and told Tracey what had happened. Our bond became stronger than it really was and a vague plan was made for our escape.

I was so glad to have my bag back with everything in it and I asked Tracey what had happened after we left. Tracey was high and enjoyed telling the story, she told us the guy Lucy had kicked didn't get up for a while. The other staff were more concerned about him than anything and were screaming and shouting in Japanese until he became conscious, then they closed the club and told everyone to leave. Tracey had seen Steve's message and grabbed our stuff from the staff room without any trouble luckily. She also felt we should get far away ASAP. It's funny how drugs work, one minute you're on top of the world, then the next you're crashing through dark feelings. Not only mentally, but physically too. I wanted more coke but at the same time knew it was a very bad idea.

In that state we decided to go to our own apartments, grab some stuff and get out of Tokyo. The biggest fear was would we be able to do it. Paranoia is like your shadow when you're high and it's always there. Sometimes you can ignore it **and other times it drives you crazy.**

Our plan was simple but risky. Leave Steve's place all together and get our stuff. It didn't feel real anymore, instead, I was floating above it all as a spectator not a participant. I was still anxious when I climbed out of the taxi and put my key in the lock of my door.

I felt immense relief seeing my door hadn't been forced open and that was a good sign. We entered carefully, quietly and ready to run with Steve leading the way. I think Steve was on a mission; he was enjoying the adventure and being the man. Once inside, I found my place was as I had left it, no one was there and nothing had been touched. Without delay we started packing things into my suitcase. I didn't have much stuff, but it's always surprising what you collect without trying.

Within about ten minutes I had all my necessities. I got changed and so did Lucy, then I grabbed some shoes and some toiletries. Last was the most important item; my treasure box. I call it that even though it's only a shoebox. I keep all my important things in there, passport, letters, cash, jewellery, insurance details and my work contract for my school which reminded me of work. What excuse could I use? They were expecting me today; so I decided to call them later.

It's funny how these days we depend on our phones so much. It was nice to have my phone in my hand again, but I didn't want to use it. I was stressed and high so I switched it off; all I wanted to do was get out of town.

"That will do everybody. Let's get to the train station." I said this to everybody, but then Lucy reminded me she needed to go to her place too. We got a taxi and found Lucy's place untouched. She packed a suitcase quickly and I think it only took about five minutes, then we said goodbye to Steve and Tracey, walked to the metro and were on our way to Tokyo station.

ON THE RUN

I was feeling a lot better by then. Surrounded by people and leaving town was on the right track. Not thinking too deeply about anything just that it was the best thing to do. Lucy looked excited and told me she was ready for a change. I withdrew some money and was happy to see I had money in the bank; probably enough for a month or two if I was careful. The metro was busy and it felt strange seeing everyone doing normal things; that had been me twenty four hours ago.

Now we were on the run. Maybe we overreacted but to this day I don't think so. The club owners lost face with their girls and some customers and I was sure they would want revenge. They were well connected and could find us if they wanted to. It might be very difficult if we left no trace of where we had gone. We told Steve and Tracey we were leaving the country which was Lucy's idea and I liked it. We got to Tokyo station and that was when I felt like we were really on the run. Every step I took felt risky, my heart was pumping hard and I felt very exposed. I couldn't help but search the faces for danger and felt on edge. **Soon we got to the ticket office,**

"Katie, are you sure about going north? We could go anywhere we want to."

"Yes we could, but for many reasons Hokkaido feels the right choice. It's far away; nobody knows us and we can work there." I said this confidently but thinking I knew nothing about Hokkaido, except it's Japan's most northern island, had great snow and famous for good food. We bought one way tickets and were on our way within half an hour.

Shinkansen is a great way to travel long distance. We were traveling at about 300kph and it felt like we were gliding on ice. It's so smooth with comfortable reclining seats and we had our own section. It was one of those golden moments of intimacy and flowing conversation. All was going well until about half way; Lucy decided to confess a few things that shocked me.

"I need to tell you something Katie." Was how it started.

"I've been dealing drugs for about two years in Tokyo now. That money Steve gave me in the bar was actually for the club owners. They have been supplying me and I give the drugs to different people. I'm telling you this because that's all going to stop from now on, although, I owe the club a lot of money. Luckily they don't know who I supply, but they will want their money back. Let's keep our heads down and everything should be okay. We also have a lot of money, their money really, but now it's ours and we earned it. Let's use it to get a place and take a holiday together."

This shocked me and made me feel scared again. Saying that, it didn't take me long to accept the money and decide it was a bonus. They had a lot of money and we needed it. The fact that Lucy had been dealing was a shock, I had never been into drugs and didn't want to start. I told her this and she reassured me that she was done with that chapter in her life. She made me laugh by describing it as, "Hanging up her scales."

I believed she could do it and told her that, they say things happen for a reason and maybe it was all fate. I could start seeing the positives of leaving Tokyo as it might do us both the world of good. I decided it was time to check my phone. There were many calls and messages from work; they seemed more worried than angry and wanted me desperately to call them.

"I'm gonna call work Lucy, what should I say?"

"How about telling them you've had an emergency and have to fly home today?"

"Okay, that sounds best." I called and was put through to the manager. She was glad to hear from me and she tried to find out more information with lots of questions. I told her nicely it was too sensitive to talk about. She also asked when I'd be back to work; that stumped me for a moment. After a pause I simply said I wouldn't be coming back and that made me start to cry.

There were also two calls from the club, no message just the calls. I decided I'd need a new phone just in case they could track me. Lucy thought that was hilarious and explained it was impossible. I deleted their contact and we promised to never answer a call from them again. The trolley lady came by and we got a mini feast of salad, rice balls, sandwiches, salami and some coffee.

The scenery was stunning. When you leave Tokyo going north, for about the first thirty minutes it's just city after city. Big complexes of apartment buildings, factories and sky scrapers, then you hit the countryside. Snow capped mountains and hills appear; many farms and rice fields. Japan is a very beautiful country and seventy percent of it is uninhabited. That's why the cities are so highly populated.

HOKKAIDO

After living on the beautiful island of Hokkaido for about three months I loved it. Hokkaido is full of wild and outstanding nature; delicious food and very hospitable people. We started by living in the main city called Sapporo. It was like most cities in Japan at first glance, but becoming more interesting the longer we stayed. What I really liked was the fact that within a thirty minute drive, you could be surrounded by breathtaking nature. Waterfalls you can hear from a far distance and make you feel the power of nature, majestic mountain ranges that spark the imagination and forests that speak of mystery.

We changed from city lovers to nature lovers and it happened quickly. There was no need to work and we enjoyed weekends full of adventure and weekdays of leisure. It was the beginning of winter and we saw the first snowfall, which we celebrated by trying to catch snowflakes with our mouths. Usually, it's the simple things that you remember the most and that is true of our Hokkaido adventure. It was our first time to snowboard and we both picked it up easily. There's nothing better than a day on the slopes finished with a good meal and a long soak in an 'onsen'.

An 'onsen' is a hot spring and Hokkaido's are rated some of the best in the world as is their powder snow. Friends were made easily and wherever we went people were kind to us. In the Japanese countryside foreigners are often a welcomed novelty.

English is Japan's second language, but most Japanese don't get many chances to use it or meet 'gaijin' (foreigners). Sometimes you notice children just staring at you or adults itching to meet you. It has to be said that in general, Japanese people are some of the nicest people on this planet. Often shy to start a relationship, but once started, they open up and you can see an innocence and honesty not often found.

We booked into a guest house on our first night in Sapporo and had our own room. The kitchen / dining room and showers were shared, luckily, that was never an issue. I always felt I had the best of both worlds because if I wanted solitude I had my room and when I wanted to socialise, I just went downstairs. There were twenty rooms and the inhabitants where a mix of nationalities. In the room next to us were a young Japanese couple. We became friends and sometimes cooked for each other. They also helped us learn Japanese and we taught them English.

Then there was Billy from Canada, what a character. Recently divorced and at a turning point in his life. He liked to both party and work hard teaching English. He was full of stories from his backpacking years and had time for anyone. I remember one night he made a cocktail party, we made some unusual cocktails and he was a great host. He organised crazy party games and lots of good food. One particular game I enjoyed was charades. You had to write down what you were doing secretly and act it out silently. I chose taking money out of an ATM and nobody could get it. Everyone liked Billy and he always made you laugh. But sadly, it was all an act. After only knowing him two months he committed suicide by jumping in front of a train. There was no suicide note or any clear reason why he did that. We went to his funeral and that was a culture shock.

Everybody was there from the guesthouse and his family had come. His ex Japanese wife and her family were there too. At a Japanese funeral everybody wears black and gives a money gift in a special envelope to the immediate family, also the night before the funeral everybody gathered for drinks. Without planning to, I drunk way too much and mixed my drinks. I woke up feeling rough but didn't let it stop me attending the ceremony. Suddenly in the middle of the ceremony I felt sick. I got up, bowed and dashed for the exit. Luckily I saw the toilets straightaway, ran in and was violently sick. After that, I washed my face and mouth then went back to the ceremony. I sat down and Lucy whispered in my ear,

"We could hear everything!" On later inspection I saw the toilet was next to the ceremony hall with a thin wall. That is the most embarrassed I've ever been in my life. Next the body was cremated after a long ceremony in the temple. This involved a lot of chanting and giving of flowers. We also saw Billy in his casket one last time and I was nearly sick again. He had been fixed the best they could but the impact must of destroyed his body and his face seemed artificial.

After the cremation the casket was put on a table and one by one we took the bones out and put them in an urn. This was done with chopsticks by passing the bones to each other in a line. Last was a formal meal with drinks and this was when we found out what Billy had been hiding.

His ex-wife made a touching speech and explained Billy had cancer. He had recently been given two years left to live all going well. She also said this was one of the reasons they divorced as he didn't want her to suffer. We were shocked and also disappointed, why hadn't he told us? We could of supported him and maybe a cure could have been found. I felt he had made a big mistake hiding this. I will always miss Billy and hope his family can move on. Me and Lucy also promised each other we would never commit suicide. Whatever the choices are, suicide is the worst choice and in many ways very selfish.

We soon moved on and those were some of the best days of our time in Japan. Lucy was happy too. She needed the lifestyle change and you could see the change in her. She looked healthier and enjoyed every day as if it was a gift. She used to say,

"Yesterday is the past and today is the present". I've never forgotten that phrase and try to live by it. There was only one bad event during our time in Hokkaido; it was in the party district area. It was about three on a Saturday morning, we'd been out partying and were pretty drunk. It was in the last bar we went to where it all went wrong. Lucy thought the barman had made a mistake with her change and after shouting at the barman, she threw the coins at him and they hit him in the face. When she got angry she was wild and unpredictable.

He pulled out a pistol from under the bar and pointed it at her face. Lucy in her wild state, leaned forwards just inches away from potential death and shouted,

"Go on then, shoot me!" I noticed the big hardened grisly faced barman's hand was not steady, and by the look on his face, he was in a rage. I tried pulling Lucy away from him but she insisted on giving him more abuse.

"That's not a real gun. Come on you asshole; SHOOT ME!" That's when my adrenaline kicked in and I literally dragged her out of the bar from behind. Once outside she started laughing and her laugh was contagious. If anyone had seen the whole scene, they would of called us crazy. Also, it was that night Lucy said,

"I've had enough of Hokkaido, it's time you met my parents. I'm sure they'll love you and we can get work in Hong Kong.

Our money's nearly gone and I want to leave. What do you think?" Without any hesitation I said yes and the next day we started planning going to Hong Kong. The more I read and heard about Hong Kong the more I wanted to go. It had always felt like a mysterious place in my mind.

HONG KONG

I was ready for the adventure and had always wanted to see Hong Kong. It was on my bucket list; but something not on my list was meeting Lucy's parents and staying with them. This was only going to be temporary until we started making money. The first time we talked about that was on the plane.

"Do your parents know about us and that we are lovers Lucy?" I had to ask.

"No way. They only know me as a good studious girl who went to Japan for work experience in my field of study which was international management, that's what I studied at my university. I learnt a lot in Japan, but none of it will look good on my resume. Can you imagine the work experience section? Talented at making old men happy, excellent sales skills with drugs and very good people skills from lots of socialising and drinking."

"You might need to re-word that, how about; lots of experience managing both finances and staff. Good at multitasking and dealing with problems. Proactive, very motivated and can work well in a team or individually." We giggled at this and then decided to make our resumes once we landed.

"Going back to my question Lucy, do you think your parents will accept us as we are? Meaning, in a relationship and in love?" This caught her of balance and it was obviously difficult for her.

"Let's tell them straightaway. This is two thousand and seventeen; they have to accept us." I agreed but started to worry about their reaction. In my eyes it could go down one of two ways. One, they accepted and supported us or two, it caused a family rift. Number two scared me as I didn't want to be the cause of that, but my love for Lucy was so strong I felt I couldn't hide it if I tried.

Hong Kong was everything I hoped for and it was a nice change from Sapporo. We both loved the excitement, the culture and the liveliness of the city. It's a city that never sleeps and is full of adventure; every district is different and there is so much to see and do. We didn't meet her family at first as they were in Sri Lanka attending to family business. We booked into a cheap hotel and filled our first week with daily trips, great food and meeting some locals.

Then the money run out for both of us. As we gave our last cash to the hotel receptionist for two more nights reality sunk in. You need money to live in any city and Hong Kong is no exception. Lucy made some calls and we got job interviews the next day at an international kindergarten where she had worked before.

I was first in and felt the interview went very well. The only uncomfortable moment was lying about the gap since my last job in Japan teaching and the lack of a reference. I told them that if they called the school they could get a good reference and I gave them a fake name and number. My thinking was if they called it's over, or if they took me on face value, all would be okay. It worked and we both signed contracts to start work in three days.

Not only did we get jobs but the school sponsored my visa and gave us a one year contract for work with a very small but cosy apartment. We moved in the next day and felt very satisfied with our accomplishments in such a short time. Also, in three days her parents were returning and there was a plan for a family gathering in a top hotel.

The job was as expected, demanding, tiring, but lots of fun and smiles; working with kindergarten age students is a challenge. You need eyes in the back of your head and lots of energy as we would be with the children from eight thirty to four thirty. The routine was simple, first circle time and play time to help set the mood. Then morning activities using English, like simulating shopping, singing, arts and crafts, picnics, travel and school subjects. Children are like sponges and learn very fast which makes it very rewarding. Saying that, there are moments when it doesn't go as planned. I remember my first art class; I showed a picture of me made using water paints, yarn, glitter and stickers on a piece of A4 paper. I asked the students to create their own self portrait using the same materials. Should be easy right?

That wasn't the case. The room looked like a bombsight after twenty minutes. Not only that, but the students decided it was more fun to paint each other than follow my example. Looking back I can laugh and it was a big lesson in teaching kids. I also remember the look on the head teachers face when she came into the classroom unexpectedly.

She was a nice lady and very serious about teaching. First, I registered shock on her face and then anger. However, together we cleaned up the best we could and I got training on how to conduct an art class. The trick is to be very organised and clear with the rules. Then, step by step you use only one material at a time. That worked and raised the level of English used in the class too. Life is full of lessons and that job helped me a lot. I remember a veteran kindergarten teacher saying to me.

"You can learn a lot from these students" I thought she was joking; did she mean picking your nose? Tying shoelaces? How to insult someone and then be their best friend? I'll never forget her next words,

"Children are not racist, sexist or any of those negative things. They can also stumble and fall, but sure enough they can pick themselves up and carry on!" We became great co-workers and **good friends.**

THE PRINCE HOTEL

Finally, the time had come to meet Lucy's parents; well actually, her parents, two brothers and some other relatives. The hotel is one of the best in Hong Kong and The Prince Hotel is both popular and famous. It has a beautiful interior, a great location and breathtaking views of the city. It is also one of the most expensive hotels in the city, a one night stay was a month's salary for me. Fortunately, Lucy's parents were paying for everything and that was when I found out her family were well off. It had never occurred to me before.

My family are wonderful back in Australia, not rich or poor, just comfortable. I love my family very much, but I hadn't spoken to them in months. At the age of twenty six though, I felt that was okay; still a call wouldn't hurt. That call went very well and they laughed about my adventures and praised me on my successes. I told them about Lucy and they wished us luck. I told them we were in love and they said congratulations. I was so relieved that this renewed my confidence in meeting Lucy's family.

Lucy was feeling good about the reunion too. Her take on it was that her family were very close and would happily accept our news. When the evening came to meet them, we both finished work at four thirty giving us an hour to get ready. I love those moments of pre-party feelings, anticipated fun, going to new places and meeting new people. As we got ready I tried to learn as much as possible about her family whilst drinking red wine and listening to The Rolling Stones. Lucy told me her father's name was Zhak Devi, her mother Linda Devi and her older brothers Tom and David.

Zhak was tall, dark and handsome, born in Sri Lanka and educated in England. A rugby fanatic and still worked in TV as a model. A kind man she said with a good sense of humour and completely in love with Linda. Apparently, it was the same for them as us, love at first sight, but in a bar in London.

Linda was born and raised in the UK, very beautiful, elegant and sophisticated. She was into fashion designing now and before that she was a model. According to Lucy, Linda wore the trousers in the family and gently guided them all. Lucy said her mother once said their marriage was like a boat ride. Zhak in the front paddling hard and feeling in control of everything, whilst Linda was guiding unseen in the back using the rudder. I liked that image very much.

As for the brothers, Tom the oldest took after his Dad in both looks and character. A keen rugby player and working in TV. David was unique she said, as he didn't take after anyone. He worked as an architect in Hong Kong and was a little shy. She said he was her favourite and they had always been close.

Before long it was time to go. We loved using the tram in Hong Kong; it's nostalgic with great views and perfect for people watching. Our tram stop was called 'The Prince Hotel' and we stepped off the tram into the night **outside the hotel.**

Lucy was looking gorgeous and she was shining. Dressed in a classic black Chanel dress that didn't leave much to the imagination, her hair held up by chopsticks with light makeup and looking very sexy. I loved it when she wore her hair up revealing her exotic neck. She smiled at me and I felt so lucky to be with her and she complemented me too.

"You look good enough to eat Katie, in fact that is exactly what I intend to do later." Then she kissed me on the lips slowly and longingly. I was wearing my new summer dress that I'd bought especially for the occasion. A little more conservative than Lucy's and that's how it usually went with us in most things.

As we entered the lobby the first thing I noticed was the space; it was huge. There was enough space for a big party and it was busy with lots of well-dressed people.

It was like being in a dream as my feet sunk into the carpet and the lighting made everything more beautiful.

"Let's get a drink Lucy." Lucy however, wasn't listening, she was staring at the big handsome man approaching us. Some people don't need props or fancy clothes to steal the show and he was one of them. He went straight up to Lucy and embraced her in a long loving hug that made her feet leave the floor. They kissed and then he was looking at me.

"You must be my daughter's best friend Katie, pleased to meet you," and he offered me his hand. I was speechless for a moment, but Zhak soon changed that.

"Come, follow me please. Everyone is waiting for us." Then we entered the elevator.

"I'm very pleased to meet you too Mr Devi." My voice sounded too loud to me and childish echoing in the elevator.

"Please call me Zhak, a friend of my daughter, is a friend of mine." His voice sounded strong, confident and well educated.

I wanted to clear the air straightaway. I thought that, if I told him we were not only friends but lovers all would be fine. Lucy read my mind. I could tell by the way she was looking at me with her frown. This happened a lot with us and sometimes it was spooky. Zhak broke the spell.

"Welcome to Hong Kong Katie! Do you like it here?"

"Yes, very much. It is everything I hoped for and much more." I could see he liked that and showed me Lucy's smile, except it was bigger and in different features. I have always loved meeting people's family and seeing the similarities.

The elevator suddenly stopped and the elevator lady announced we had arrived at the Imperial suite which was a 'Wow factor'. The most amazing room I've ever seen, just the city views took my breath away. In the centre, was an elegant large wooden table fit for royalty and surrounding it was the King's family. The Queen was Linda and she quickly left the table and came to us. Like a mother who hasn't seen her daughter for a lifetime, she held Lucy at arm's length and looked at her smiling for what seemed ages. Then they hugged and kissed. She ignored me at first or at least it felt that way. You could see the emotions and the love from Linda for her daughter. You could also see they were mother and daughter in height, build and style. Finally, she turned to me and kissed me lightly on the cheek.

"Hello Katie, I'm so pleased to finally meet you. Lucy talks about you all the time and I can see why; you are very beautiful."

"Not as beautiful as you Linda."

"You are too kind Katie."

She had a lovely voice and very British. High society British and it sounded like music to me. Next, the two brothers approached and Linda introduced us, they were both very warm and friendly. They embraced their sister at the same time and I could see the bond, they all laughed together which was a little eerie because they all laughed the same way, with their heads back and that long loud contagious laugh. I wish I could do that; I've tried in private a few times and failed, it just isn't me.

I was guided to the table and introduced to Zhak's brother and his son. We were shown our seats and everybody sat down. Sometimes I get a strong feeling I need a drink, I'd had it earlier in the lobby and it hit me again. At that moment a waiter approached with a tray of wine and juice.

"Would madam like a beverage before dinner?" I thanked him and took a glass of red, then I thought to myself, take it easy tonight and everything will be fine. You're with good people, so relax and enjoy a wonderful evening.

The conversation flowed as we all enjoyed drinks and the excellent food. The food was to die for. The first course was a large dish of Chinese dumplings. Each dipped in a soya based spicy sauce just before popping the whole thing in your mouth. You have to eat them whole or the juice will go everywhere, (as I had learnt on previous attempts). The conversation was 'catch-up time', everybody had stories and they were going one by one around the table. When it was my turn I told them about how much we had enjoyed Japan and I managed to avoid all the crazy parts. I painted a picture of two people enjoying Japan for all its cultural points. I told them about teaching too and how much I enjoyed it.

The next dish was braised eggplants and they melted in your mouth. At this point we heard about Tom's newest girlfriend. He confessed to being madly in love and felt she was the one. Everyone wished him luck and hinted they'd like to meet her.

The third course was my favourite dish, Peking duck and when it's done well it's amazing. You only need a little and it is truly fit for Kings and Queens. The focus was on Lucy at this point and she didn't let us down. She told everyone how happy she was and had them crying with laughter. She also sang my praises and made me blush. I think that was where she over did it; because, after a hiking story about us, David finally spoke,

"So, when are you two getting married?" There was an awkward silence broken by Lucy.

"David you are the most intuitive man I know, how did you know? Everybody, I have some big news, Katie and me are madly in love. Also, to answer your question David, I plan on asking Katie to marry me, if she will have me that is. Does anyone object?"

That awkward silence again, this time broken by her mother. Linda stood up and raised her glass.

"I'd like to make a toast if that's possible? You are both wonderful and I'd like to make a toast to the both of you." Everybody stood up,

"To Lucy and Katie!"

"To Lucy and Katie." Everybody cheered.

I started crying as I stumbled to Linda and simply whispered in her ear,

"Thank you." Then I took a deep breath and said to everyone,

"Thank you everybody so much for accepting us. We do love each other very much, and Lucy, my answer is YES!" Everybody cheered again.

The rest of the evening was the best time ever. I realised how worried I'd been about that moment, all for nothing! They were genuinely happy for us and I had a new family. This was all happening so fast but it felt right. The food didn't matter anymore, except that last course of pavlova. It was incredible and has become our number one dessert ever since.

ROOFTOP GARDEN

That night when I met Lucy's family and said yes to marriage will always stay in my memory as one of the best nights of my life. Sometimes dreams do come true and true love conquers all. The next thing we did was to start planning the wedding. Our first idea was to write down separately what kind of wedding we'd like; once that was done we shared our ideas.

The first topic on our lists was location. I wrote garden and Lucy wrote rooftop, so we agreed on a rooftop garden wedding in Hong Kong. We both wanted a small wedding and the total number of guests was sixty. Rings were easy for us and we found exactly what we wanted in the first shop we went in; two Asian gold rings. We also discussed budget. Lucy surprised me by saying her father wanted to pay for everything; including my parent's flights and travel costs. This generosity was hard for me and my family to accept. Then Zhak visited us one night and that was it. He convinced us there was no compromising on his request to pay for everything.

Dresses were the hardest part for both of us; it took weeks of searching and trying different dresses and ideas. In the end we both liked the same dress, a beautiful and simple cream coloured vintage dress. We decided to vary them by mine having long sleeves, touching the floor and with a covered back. Lucy's would have short sleeves, to her knees and an open back. I felt these dresses expressed a lot about us as individuals.

We found a great wedding agent and the second location she showed us was perfect. It was a rooftop sixty floors up and we loved it at first sight. It had two bars, a dance floor and an open air chapel. There was no garden but that could be made for us ... and it was.

The big day was decided and guests

were invited. Everyone we invited replied with congratulations and promises of attendance. We chose our garden with white roses everywhere, pine trees, bushes and lots of floral decoration. Some people say a wedding is one of the biggest stresses in a lifetime; I disagree. I enjoyed the planning so much and it got me excited every time. Lucy enjoyed it too and I realised that we were both quite easily pleased. We were getting more and more excited as the big day got closer. My parents and my best friend Helen were arriving the next day and all was set.

I had the day off work to pick them up and take them to their hotel. It was a nice hotel, nothing like the Prince Hotel, but I hoped they would like it because it was close to us and had good reviews. Countdown to the big day had begun with only three days to go. We had a meal booked for the parents to meet and Saturday would be a day of sightseeing, then our wedding on Sunday at noon.

The next morning I woke super early and jumped out of bed wide awake. I felt like a little girl on christmas day full of excitement and expectations. We decided to have our favourite breakfast downstairs in a Chinese dumpling restaurant. These are where the locals go, they are noisy, friendly and the menu is mouthwatering. We had all kinds of Chinese dumplings sat at a big round table with about six strangers. They enjoyed our company and together we ate well. Once we were full, we went to the airport and eagerly awaited the arrival of my parents and Helen.

"Tell me Katie, what are your parents like and who is Helen?"

"Well, my mum, Julie, is bit of a hippy. She loves music and is an active environmentalist; she is a very good artist too. She raised me well and always taught me to respect everything and everyone.

Bill my Dad is a classic Aussie. Lovely guy, very easy going, loves his sport, beer and the BBQ. He's in the mining business and I think he will get on well with your dad.

Helen you'll love; but hopefully not too much!" I joked.

"She's a beauty in every way and we have been best friends since primary school. I'm so happy they are coming, although it might be a culture shock for them at first, I'm sure they'll enjoy everything."

Then we saw them exit the terminal and I relived that special moment of meeting loved ones after some time apart. I love my family dearly and often felt guilty about not seeing them as much as I'd like to. As for Helen, she has her own life now and whenever we meet it's a blast. We formed a circle and introductions were made. Dad was first to break the ice.

"Congratulations you two! We are happy for you and looking forward to the party! Is it a Barbie wedding?" This confused Lucy for a moment and I was laughing as I translated.

"He means, are we having a BBQ at the wedding Lucy." Good old Dad, never a dull moment when he's around. We had good news for him because we had included a BBQ in the wedding day plan. Lucy told him this and you could see his smile from a mile away! We all hugged and Mum was next.

"Welcome to the family darling and we are so pleased to meet you. I can see why Katie fancies you, and Katie had better watch out, I might steal you away from her." We all laughed at this and then Helen said,

"Funny though Katie, after all these years I've known you and you've never made any advances on me!" Again everybody was laughing. I didn't know how to respond to that so I changed the topic.

"Let's get going shall we or would you like to rest?" My dad laughed at that and boomed,

"No bloody way. We want to see Hong Kong, how about we go to the hotel first, freshen up and then hit the town?" We all agreed and it was so nice to see them all again, especially out of their comfort zone. This was going to be the trip of a lifetime for them all. This was the first time in Asia for all of them and I was determined to make it the best it could be.

Our hometown is a small town in New South Wales. It's a very beautiful part of the world and the nature is similar to Hokkaido in many ways. It was also completely different to Hong Kong. In our town everybody knew each other and the biggest night out was the Sports Bar. That said though, my life there had been wonderful. Sometimes suffocating and that's one of the reasons why I left, I needed more and I'd found it. At that moment, I realised my concept of home had changed dramatically.

THE ALBION

The Albion was their hotel for two weeks. Their rooms were next to each other and the hotel was modern and very clean. The reception staff spoke English and were very helpful. I got the impression they enjoyed meeting us and wanted our stay to be the best it could be. Once settled in, me and Lucy left them to refresh and told them we'd be back at six to take them out. Tomorrow was the meeting of the parents and tonight was our time together.

When we got back to the Albion at six Dad was in the lobby. It was an unusual lobby with lots of freaky modern art on the walls and it was also well equipped. There was a pool table, lots of black leather couches, a bar and that's where my dad was. He'd already made friends with some other men and didn't see us come in. You can hear him in a crowded room above everyone else usually and today was no different.

"I like your dad!" Lucy whispered in my ear.

"That makes two of us, he likes you too chubby cheeks." With that Lucy crept up behind him and tapped him on the shoulder. He turned around, smiled and took Lucy's hands.

"Ah, my girlfriend is here. Are you ready for wining and dining tonight? Ohh! And who's your beautiful friend?"

"The agency said you requested two young ladies tonight sir!" I replied and we all laughed. He bid farewell to his new friends who looked confused about the situation, then Dad led us to the elevator.

"Let's go see if your mum and Helen are ready shall we?" We went to his room first and Mum opened the door. She always looks good and that night she looked stunning. She kissed all of us and welcomed us into their room.

After a few minutes I left Lucy with them and went next door for Helen. She was ready, however after opening the door she asked me to come in.

"It's good to see you again Katie and you look so happy! I want you to know we were all surprised at first with your news. But we all agreed love is love and if this is what you want, then we all support you. I can clearly see the love and friendship you have together. Congratulations and I hope your dreams come true." This touched my heart and I said through tears,

"I love you Helen. That means so much to me and thank you so much for coming!" We had a long hug with a quick chat and then went to get the others.

"Hi everybody! Do you like this hotel?" I asked the group and they all agreed it was a great choice. Everyone was hungry so we took them to one of the most popular tourist spots in Hong Kong called 'Victoria

Peak'. It's a mountain that looks over Hong Kong and the views are mesmerizing, also at night it looks magnificent. There's a very good Chinese restaurant on the top and we enjoyed good food with even better conversation. Once we'd finished eating and drinking we took the cable car down and hit the town. We all love a drink and there are plenty of good bars and restaurants. We got a bit drunk and by twelve decided to call it a night. Dad **convinced us all to have a final drink in their hotel.**

We had some drinks with his new mates and a few of the hotel's staff joined us. The party finished around two in the morning and everyone said goodnight. Helen wanted something from the convenience store downstairs and we said goodnight at the elevator doors. I didn't see any trouble coming, but what occurred later on shocked me.

It was seven in the morning when my dad called me, telling me Helen was in his room and she was in shock. He asked us to come right away and we got there thirty minutes later to hear Helen's story. She didn't remember going to her room and her last memory was being given a drink from a European businessman in the hotel.

When she woke up that morning she was naked and he was on top of her; also naked. She'd screamed which made him run out of the room with his clothes in his hands. She had put on her dressing gown and come to Mum and Dad's room. Dad had gone looking for him, but to no avail which personally I was happy about, my dad might of done something he would've regretted later. Helen was all clenched up and couldn't calm down.

"I think he drugged and raped me!" She was crying and all I could do at first was hold her tightly. Lucy gently suggested getting a medical check at the hospital, Helen agreed to go with Lucy and me by taxi.

After the check the doctor confirmed she was clear which was a very big relief; she hadn't been raped. When we got back to the hotel my dad was furious and wanted to kill the man. He'd been looking for him and had involved the staff. Nobody had seen anything and Katie couldn't describe him clearly. The situation was escalating with my dad, so we decided the best thing to do was change hotels. We packed their belongings and went looking for a new hotel.

The new hotel turned out to be better with much nicer rooms, a rooftop swimming pool and a small gym. Helen asked us to put it all in the past and not let it ruin the holiday. She said it could've been a lot worse and she felt she had learnt a big lesson. It's sad that some people would do such a thing and you have to be so careful these days.

The day went better than expected and we travelled around by tram seeing the sights. I enjoyed seeing Hong Kong through their eyes and the things that had become normal for me were sometimes shocking for them.

Hong Kong abuses all your senses. The tastes are very varied and usually amazing. Sometimes an aroma will come which is hard to place. It could be anything, from fermenting tofu to drying seafood in the sun. The sights are everywhere, from semi naked men working to high flyers in sports cars. Old buildings held up by bamboo next to a classic colonial building. Hong Kong is a noisy city too and I enjoyed sometimes just listening to the city with my eyes closed. When city planners designed the city I think they were high, but it works. Hong Kong is the old and the new blended together by a master.

The sun started setting and it was time to brush up for the evening's special event, the meeting of the families at Lucy's parent's home. We all went our own ways and planned to meet at seven outside their hotel.

"Are you nervous about tonight Lucy?" I asked once in the comfort of our room.

"No, I think it will be a night to remember and our families should get on well, I wouldn't be surprised if Tom hits on Helen, she seems just his type."

"That would be interesting, I've only known her to have one boyfriend and they were inseparable for about four years. They broke up a year ago; so she might be interested." Getting ready was always fun for us, a little music, some wine and happy conversation. Once ready we went to pick them up. They were happy with their hotel and we all had a gin and tonic made by Dad in my parent's room.

After stepping out of their hotel Lucy directed us to a big surprise with a hand gesture, a beautiful black shining limousine with a chauffeur waiting for us. I'd never been in a limousine before and I got excited. It was a big surprise for me and my family seeing a limousine for us. Lucy saw the look on our faces and laughed,

"Looks like my dad is going all out for you guys tonight."

"That's fine with us sweetie. In fact, I could very easily get used to this way of travelling in Hong Kong." My dad said this to everybody, including the chauffeur holding his door open. The drive was fun and a great experience, drinking champagne and feeling like Cinderella going to the ball. **The big difference was I had my lover already with me and my family were the opposite to wicked.**

Their home was stunning. Once through the big iron security gates you could see the front of it. A classic British colonial house and I was shocked, not only at the size and beauty, but that Lucy had never told me her family lived like this. Not hurt, just curious why she'd never told me she came from money. It was three floors supported by large pillars and the big arched windows made the effect complete. Then there was the surrounding grounds, full of tropical greenery, a sparkling pool and a very deep green lawn. We were met by a well dressed butler who looked Chinese and had a very British accent. He was a handsome man and you could see his connection with Lucy was very strong, like a loving uncle.

"This is Mr Chang, my favourite man in

the world." Lucy said with pride.

"Well thank you kindly Lucy, and just for the record, you are my favourite girl in the world!"

"How are you doing Mr Chang?"

"Always better when I see your lovely smile."

"You always say that and I love it!"

Lucy introduced us all and Mr Chang gently kissed all the ladies on the hand. I hadn't seen that done for a long time **and thought it was cute.**

The evening was a big success with everyone in the mood for socialising and everybody made it special. I was curious if Tom would be on Helen's case, however they hardly talked. David was with her more and I could see the chemistry between them, they were animated together and looked very close. Just as I had predicted, my dad and Zhak got on like a house on fire, making jokes and sometimes teaching us rugby chants which was hilarious. Linda and my mum were doing grand too. They are both talented artists and were often seen in deep conversation. At one point in the evening I was alone with Lucy.

"Sorry Lucy, we haven't had any time for ourselves tonight."

"Don't worry, we will have all the time in the world after tomorrow!"

"Can you believe it's come so fast?"

"I know what you mean. By the way, the weather is looking good for us."

"That is fabulous news." We had been having this conversation almost every day. If the weather played up it would greatly affect our plans for a rooftop garden wedding. Plan B was in a big hall in the same hotel, however for me that sounded disappointing compared to our dream wedding.

"Katie, I've decided that I'm not coming home tonight, my mum said it's traditional for us to be separate on the last night before our wedding."

"That is a wedding tradition and I think we should do it." I said this with conviction and straightaway the idea appealed to me. This would make the grand entrance work well plus give me the morning with my family and Helen.

"I think everything is ready Katie, I've got my dress, the rings and new shoes. The agent called me today to confirm all is ready there; it took her about thirty minutes to get through the list and she's more stressed than us." This made me laugh as we had it easy. I suddenly wanted to ask.

"Why did you never tell me your family lived like this Lucy?"

"It's a long story, but in a nutshell, I was in love once before with a man. Sadly, it turned out he wasn't in love with me. He was in love with what he could get from me and my family financially. So, naturally I've hidden my family's wealth from everybody since then. With you though, the longer I left it, the harder it became to tell you. I'm sorry Katie!"

I took her in my arms and forgave everything. I appreciated her honesty and could understand her secrecy.

For the last part of the night we all went out on the balcony and enjoyed light snacks, drinks and talked about the wedding. We'd decided not to have a honeymoon straightaway because we wanted to enjoy Hong Kong with my parents and Helen. Our families made a few excursion plans together for museums, art exhibitions and even rugby. It was a lovely evening and friendships were made. We were driven home by Mr Chang who told us funny stories about Lucy as a little girl. Apparently, she had been a wild child which didn't surprise me. Helen stayed with me that night and fell asleep in my bed after some drinking and girls talk.

THE WEDDING

It was strange at first waking up and seeing Helen's face in front of mine. It took me a moment to get my bearings and remember why Helen not Lucy was sleeping in my bed. I had a mini panic attack thinking I might have overslept; as it turned out it was **seven** in the morning. The big day had finally come and I was getting married at noon. I planned on being there first, welcoming the guests and getting them seated. After that, we could all wait together on the rooftop for Lucy and her parents. I looked out of the window and saw the sun shining and blue skies which made me very happy.

There aren't many days in life that have a build up like a wedding. On top of that you've got so many factors. Will the guests come and enjoy the day? Will the weather be good and the sun shine? Will my speech go well? The speech was kind of formed in my head and I had thought about it a lot.

Every time I practiced it in my head or out loud it changed a little and I was sure each change was an improvement. I wanted it to be honest, funny and hopefully, touching. I had three key words in this order: Family, friends and love. I also wanted to express how lucky I felt about everything and finish with a big thank you.

I made some tea for me and Helen and put the radio on. I was a little hung over from the day before, but knew a hot shower would fix that. Sure enough, a long soak in the shower woke me up. I practiced my speech in the shower and felt it was as good as it could be. I woke Helen up and we enjoyed breakfast together reminiscing about the good times we'd had in Australia. There were so many good times and it's funny how you forget some stories.

One funny story Helen helped me to remember was our first road trip. I'd told my family I was staying at Helen's, and she'd told her family she was at mine. We went to the highway and hitchhiked all the way to Brisbane. Jumping in a strangers truck or car is risky, but we made it in a day with three different lifts. Being picked up didn't take long and luckily nothing bad happened. It was a great adventure and we met some interesting characters. At fifteen years old we wanted to do everything.

The first night we made out with two surfers all in the same room. We met them on the beach and got drunk on their cheap wine. They were nice guys and didn't mind that we didn't have any money. They supplied everything and thought both of us were eighteen years old, because that's what Helen had told them. That was our first time to smoke weed, they rolled the joints and showed us how to enjoy the relaxed feeling. I remember at some points of the night laughing so much it hurt. What everybody was laughing about I can't clearly remember, but it was a very memorable night in other ways.

Helen helped me get ready for the wedding as we danced around to music and it didn't take long. I took a final look in the mirror and liked what I saw, the dress fitted me well, my hair was up and just a little make up. It was a special morning together and we were ready to be picked up at ten thirty. Mr Chang came on time and took us to the Rooftop garden and we were the first people there, well except for the staff and the stressed agent. I had to comfort her and we practiced slow breathing techniques together.

The first job for me was to do a rehearsal with the celebrant. She was very kind and we went through the whole ceremony in about twenty minutes. The DJ was ready and I could smell food cooking on the BBQ. The photographer arrived and he had lots of requests, so I basically followed his advice, he also had a wicked sense of humour and made me laugh a lot. Helen was our flower girl and would lay a pathway of rose petals for Lucy's entrance.

The guests started arriving and it was overwhelming for me at times to see all these lovely people here to celebrate our marriage. Some I knew and some I didn't, but we all had one thing in common, we were there to celebrate and I wanted it to be a party to be remembered. Everything was in place and soon it was time for Lucy to arrive.

She was fashionably late, apparently not intentionally; city traffic. When she did arrive, the rooftop doors slowly slid open to reveal Lucy with her parents either side. She looked so beautiful and there was something else, a touch of innocence. Something I didn't see much in Lucy, however, it looked good on her at that moment. Helen stepped in front of her and laid the petals followed by Lucy and her parents. I waited and realised my hands were shaking from nerves. Soon the ceremony began and it went fast and smooth. It was magical and everything was perfect. After we had made our vows and kissed we started the party, actually Lucy started it by shouting into the mic,

"Let's get pissed!"

The music was playing, drinks started flowing and the party was in full swing. Next were the photos and it was strange having photos taken constantly for an hour. There were small breaks, but I soon found out that being famous was not for me. I planned on not getting drunk as I wanted to talk with everybody. There were so many great conversations and I managed to chat with nearly everybody. Before I knew it, I was told it was speech time. I was first, then Lucy and finally, Helen.

Speech time was announced and everyone looked at the head table. I got up and I was ready.

"Hello everybody! Thank you so much for coming today and being a part of our special day! I feel so emotional looking at you all. It might be easier if you all turn around and just listen please." Everybody quietly chuckled.

" You know I'm kidding, well partly. This is truly the greatest day of my life, of our lives! Did you all know that this time last year, none of this was possible in Hong Kong. The government only this year acknowledged LGBT rights. That's unbelievable really for such a diverse place. There is still much to be done in the world for equality." This got a clap and a cheer from everybody.

"It's so good that our families accepted us and for this I want to say a very big thank you! I always knew my dad was gay." Laughter again. I was on a roll!

"But seriously, we feel lucky to have you not only here, but supporting us for the rest of our lives....financially!" More laughter.

"Also to our friends both old and new. We love you and never be a stranger is our request. Let's keep our friendship forever. Especially for Lucy as she only has one friend." **Lucy laughed the most at this one.**

"Finally, Thank you Lucy for being you, making us and I promise to be yours till death do us part; unless you fuck up!" Not so much laughter for that one.

"Lucy, I love you more and more now and forever. Let's enjoy this life wherever it may go. I'd like to make a toast everybody. To family, friends and love!"

"To family, friends and love". I can remember feeling very happy and relieved once my speech was over.

Next was Lucy and her speech blew me away. It was full of interesting stories and made people laugh hysterically at some points. She also made them cry with some very honest stories. Then it was Helen's speech with funny stories and lots of positivity about same-sex marriage. After the speeches a space was made for dancing and the DJ was awesome. I love wedding parties and I danced with different people all night. The food was very good and by the end of the night my dream had come true. I was married and in heaven with Lucy.

PARADISE

That night after going home together we made love slowly like never before. The wedding was finally over, not only was it done, but we were confident it was a success. We were now married and our life together was just beginning. All our guests had a good time and nothing went wrong, so many things could have spoiled the day. You hear horror stories of fights and fires at weddings or last minute jitters and missing brides or grooms. In some countries, you hear of wedding suicide bombings, what a tragic thing to happen.

We woke up late and had a lazy morning, both of us had two weeks off work which felt really good. Our plan was to continue being tour guides and making sure everyone had a good time.

"What time are we meeting everyone?"

Was Lucy's first question of the day.

"No plan today sweet cheeks because it's is our special day. We don't have to do anything or go anywhere, if we don't want to." As I said that it felt good, I was enjoying being the host but it was tiring.

"How about staying in bed all day?"

"That sounds perfect Lucy, but please use the toilet when you need to go. I don't want to lay in a wet bed!" Lucy thought that was hilarious and started tickling me.

"This is paradise Katie and dreams do come true. Can you believe it was only a few months ago we were on the run."

"Please don't remind me, I sometimes have nightmares about those scary guys." I thought about those days often, I felt we were safe in Hong Kong and probably they had forgotten about us by now. I started thinking about the future and realised we hadn't really talked about long term plans.

"Do you think we will stay in Hong Kong

forever?" I asked Lucy this question and didn't know what to expect.

"We could do that, but something tells me we should try and see the world together. We could go anywhere, how about teaching in Thailand?"

That surprised me at first, but the idea grew on me quickly. After thinking of the pros and cons of a few countries, we decided Thailand could be our honeymoon destination whilst looking at the possibility of working there.

The next week was so much fun. Everyday different places and some of them new for us too. Helen had done her Hong Kong homework and found some real gems we didn't even know about. The best one for me was the fisherman's island.

To get there you use a cable car and for about forty minutes you are high in the sky. You can see Hong Kong one side and mountains on the other. It has a time slip feeling once you get to the island because everything is old and weather beaten. It's a small island full of history and surprises. The buildings are mostly built on stilts on the edge of the river and the bay. Fishing and tourism are the main industries and you can see signs of that everywhere.

I remember sitting on the terrace of an old restaurant overlooking the river, the food was really fresh seafood and very tasty. We watched fisherman fixing their nets, children playing by the water and housewives busy with their chores. Everything seemed so simple and tranquil. Life can be enjoyed in many different ways and I strongly felt that afternoon that simple best suited me. After that trip we planned to go to Macau. That would be just me and Lucy as our families with Helen had their own plans for sightseeing. We called it our first short honeymoon.

MACAU

To get to Macau you have three choices; plane, ferry or the new bridge. The most popular is the ferry and there are two types of ferry, the regular or the rapid. The new way to get to Macau which started this year is the bridge. It was completed after taking twelve years to build and eighteen lives of workers. This earned it the nickname 'The Bridge of Death.' It is a magnificent sight and is the longest bridge in the world, for now.

We took the regular ferry and enjoyed it very much. We got seats in the front and watched the islands go by, then after about twenty minutes we could see Macau in the distance. We were excited, but not as excited as the young guy next to us. My guess was he was so on edge that he was an addicted gambler in his twenties. He was sat on the edge of his seat the whole way noisily chewing gum. His eyes were bulging and he was constantly fidgeting.

Macau is a gambler's paradise and one of the gambling capitals of the world. The location is perfect and very beautiful. Macau used to be the Asian hub for trade, but not anymore. Now, it is the hub for fun. Gambling is banned in many Asian countries, but that doesn't mean it doesn't happen. In Japan you can find casinos if you want to, as long as you don't mind dealing with the underworld.

As we approached Macau my excitement grew. We were there for only two days, but I felt that was enough. I'd searched for things to do and there was a lot. Of course the casinos had to be seen and I wanted to learn about the islands history.

We got off the ferry and in a taxi to our hotel. The Pearl was both a hotel and a casino. We went to our room and unpacked; the room was very posh with high ceilings, plush carpet and fittings obviously chosen by an interior designer with taste. After a shower we made love, got dressed and talked about the day.

"What's the time Katie?"

"Lunchtime! Are you hungry? I hoped the answer would be yes.

"Bloody starving! What about looking for somewhere near here to eat? I saw lots of places on the way."

"Okay. Then how about a quick flutter in the casino?" I wasn't a big gambler, but loved the buzz of a casino, plus, I'd never been to a casino with Lucy.

"I've been looking forward to watching you win lots of money Katie."

We found a cute looking local restaurant with an English menu that was busy which is always a good sign. There was one spare table and we got it, the food was excellent and we enjoyed local spicy noodles. Then we took a walk around town. The town centre is an interesting mix of old and new and for some reason most of the shops sell expensive jewellery; there was gold and expensive pieces everywhere. We did some window shopping and decided it was time to try our luck on the casino tables.

Our hotel's big casino seemed the best choice and we cashed up one hundred US dollars in chips. Not a lot, but we decided it was okay to lose it. We walked around the casino first, watching the different games and players. What a great place for people watching, there were serious unsmiling players, young dudes showing off and old people enjoying the atmosphere.

"Can we try poker first Lucy?"

"I don't know how to play it, so how about I watch you play and clean up?"

"Okay. Let's go win some cash." I wasn't sure of the procedure so went to a vacant seat and sat down smiling at everyone. The dealer looked at me and asked if I had a reservation; I didn't, so he told me to get one at the entrance. A little embarrassed I made my way to the poker area entrance and saw the pit boss watching me.

"Hi! Can I make a reservation with you for table two please?"

"Certainly, please write your name here and we'll call you soon." I signed the paper and we went to the bar for a beer. After waiting about ten minutes I was called to the table. I went back to the same table and sat down. Opposite me was a young man who looked unfriendly with a very pretty lady and nobody was smiling, but all were smoking and some were winning with big piles of chips. The chips were all big numbers and I felt very small putting my one hundred dollars in front of me. The dealer looked at my chips, then at me with disdain.

"This table is a minimum of five hundred dollars, are you playing with us or not?" I was shocked and very embarrassed at the same time. My throat went dry and I apologised to everyone. I also wished them luck which was completely ignored by all. I left the table and found Lucy talking to some stranger. She hadn't seen what had just happened and I was pleased about that.

"They want a minimum of five hundred dollars to play on these tables Lucy!"

"Screw that! That's a good night out on the town, why don't we try blackjack. By the way, this is Jeff." Jeff was a good looking guy, I guessed Chinese and around thirty. He was well dressed and had a nice smile.

"Blackjack is my favourite game ladies, why don't we try our luck together?" His English was good and I felt nothing wrong with his suggestion.

"Sure, let's find our lucky table." Was my reply. With that he led the way and stopped at a blackjack table with two players absorbed in their game. One player was a very old pretty Chinese looking lady with a huge pile of chips in front of her and the other player was a middle aged western looking man. He welcomed us to join and we did. The first thing to be said on the table was,

"You, wait! Lucky three not yet." This was the old lady and without hesitation I trusted her opinion. We waited and watched for about three games until she gestured at the seat,

"You play now!" The minimum bet was fifty dollars so this meant we had two chances only. I laid down fifty dollars and we all bet against the dealer who bust. I remember the loud thumping of my heart which was an unusual feeling, it was an adrenaline party out of my control. I continued to bet all my chips and we continued to win for about six games in a row until the old lady stopped the game,

"You stop now. Go home!" Normally, I don't like words of force, but it felt right to stop. I looked at Lucy who was suffering from drop jaw,

"We've got two choices babe! We continue win or lose, or we use this money for the best night we could of hoped for."

"Let's go party!" Was Lucy's immediate reply and so we did. I thanked everybody at the table and gave them all a high five. Jeff took my seat and we wished him luck.

I was on cloud nine as I walked to the

cashier which was a first for me. I always left a casino with less than I walked in with. Not that night though; and it felt really good. Casinos can suck you dry and they are pros at that. To have one up on them was a very good feeling.

We collected our winnings which was a total of one thousand dollars. With that we had a great meal, some clothes shopping, a few hours in a night club and all wrapped up by a ninety minute foot oil massage. I couldn't have felt better and we still had money left over.

The next day started early and we made our plans over room service breakfasts. It's a great way to spoil yourself in the morning, especially when it's served in bed. I had a full English and Lucy had a continental.

"This is the best breakfast ever." I mumbled with a mouthful of eggs and bacon.

"You can say that again." Lucy replied. So I did and was treated to a light punch.

After breakfast, we slowly got ready and

checked out at ten. They let us leave our bags in reception and that left us nine hours in Macau. We took the bus to the hotspots where we enjoyed a cathedral what is actually a ruin, but still very beautiful and something to spark the imagination. The front wall is all that stands of St Paul's. You can still enjoy the rest, but it is the standing structure that reminds you of the beauty and power of a cathedral. After that was the Macau museum.

We learnt that Macau had been a Portuguese colony for four hundred years which explained the beautiful architecture. The history is fascinating and Macau is rich in both stories and wealth. During the seventh century, some five thousand slaves lived in Macau, in addition to two thousand Portuguese and twenty thousand Chinese. Just thinking about that drives my imagination wild.

"How about trying our luck in the casino again Katie?" Lucy surprised me with that as I didn't want to go there again.

"I'd much rather enjoy walking around

the town with you Lucy. There's an old Chinese building I really want to see called the Mandarin House."

"Okay, and I'm getting hungry!"

"You are always hungry! I wonder what's available around here?"

We left the museum and found ourselves in the backstreets; I love leaving the beaten tourist track. Instantly, we were surrounded by old buildings where local people lived. There were sounds of dishes being washed, hushed conversation and music. There was also a very appealing smell of food.

We found the source of this from a little cafe. We could see it was popular and the owner ushered us in. We ordered a variety of Dim Sum and they were very tasty. No trip to that part of the world is complete without an egg tart. light crispy pastry filled with egg custard. They were fresh, warm, amazing and easy to eat. After lunch we went to the Mandarin House.

The Mandarin House is very beautiful and once inside the first impression is the escapism. It's a very serene house where you can wander from room to room, through the courtyard, and up and down between the floors. It was like being in the elegant home of a wealthy Mandarin during the last days of the old Imperial Chinese. But because the mandarin worked with and studied Westerners, the house was an interesting blend of Chinese and European, like so much else in Macau. It's also very cool and a nice break from the heat and busy streets.

"I'd like a home like this one day!" Lucy said in a dreamy state.

"Me too, life would be very happy with a home like this. We should talk about that Lucy. The first thing is where shall we make our base?"

"Hong Kong would be my first choice; followed by Australia or Thailand which we won't know about for sure until after our honeymoon." This made sense to me and Hong Kong was fun. We had work and now we were married, I could get a spousal visa easily.

"Living in Hong Kong for a while sounds good to me, then maybe after that, we could try living in Australia."

"Sounds perfect Katie."

Making decisions was very easy for us. We never had fights and it felt like living in paradise still. It was soon time to catch the ferry back. We got our luggage and left Macau with smiles on our faces. That was until we got to the ferry terminal; it was madness. Nobody could explain what was happening in English and we could tell something was wrong. It turned out to be just a delay, but the staff looked stressed out and didn't want to help us. We did the only logical thing and followed the crowd. Finally, we were on the ferry going home and watched Macau fade away in the sunset.

HOME

We got home late and tired, but very satisfied with our time in Macau. The next day was a family day in Hong Kong. It was nice to be home again; to be able to slip into our own bed and find the food or drinks that we liked and I felt that this could be our home for the unforeseen future.

We slept very well that night and in the morning we were soon reunited with my family.

"How did it go on your own?" I asked this hoping for a positive answer, and I got one from Mum.

"This city is amazing! So much to see and do. Every corner reveals something new and interesting.

"What the plan for today?" Dad asked excitedly. He looked like a school boy on his first big trip.

"If it's okay, can we go to the old fish market by tram?" This was from Helen. Everybody agreed and nodded approval.

Traveling by tram in my humble opinion is the best way to see Hong Kong. We got window seats on the top deck and enjoyed the view. The city was alive and it was ten in the morning. We saw locals working inside and outside shop fronts with tourists walking leisurely enjoying the sights and the food; Hong Kong is a foodies paradise.

We got off at the old fish market and straight away it seemed like a different world. I'd never had so many weird and wonderful smells or sights hit my senses in such a short time. Rows of shops selling all kinds of seafood. Lots of dried goods that made my family laugh. Starfish, sea cucumbers and shark fins to mention a few. Shop workers invited us to buy them, but some things are not suitable souvenirs. I could imagine my family visiting their friends and giving them those strange looking foods.

Lunch was enjoyed in a very old Chinese restaurant. The Peking duck melted in your mouth and the crispy outer gave you a burst of flavour, they also gave us lots of vegetables. If you're not careful, you can end up eating unhealthily in Hong Kong. The vegetables were fried and a little oily, but I felt they still did us some good.

After the old fish market we went to the harbour and the views from there were incredible. Watching boats floating around with the city in the background and traditional Chinese junk boats with their red sails and tales of old. Hong Kong's history fascinates me, Hong Kong as we know it today, was born when China's Qing dynasty government was defeated in the First Opium War in eighteen forty two, when it ceded Hong Kong island to Britain. It was also inhabited in the Stone Age.

There is always something happening around the harbour area. The street performers are usually impressive and I also like watching people there with groups practicing all sorts of different things. One group of young ladies next to us were practicing techno music moves and we also saw some guys practicing martial arts. For the evening we had a plan to eat at our home and it was nice to have visitors. The only problem was the lack of space; Helen said she felt like Alice in Wonderland in our place. We made salad and a curry which all went down well with the wine. Dessert was egg tarts and they were devoured in minutes.

Conversation was fluid and I remember at one point Mum asking about our future plans. They got excited when we said Australia was in the plan. Sharing a nice evening at home made me think about going back to Australia, it could work, as long as Lucy was there. That's when I had the thought that for me home wasn't a building anymore. For me it was being with Lucy.

For the last few days of my parent's stay we enjoyed day trips around Hong Kong. It was a special time and we made lots of good memories together. Helen had to leave first due to work commitments. We promised to keep in touch and both cried at the airport. Then, it was time to say goodbye to my parents. They said they really enjoyed the trip and had already decided they would come again.

After they had left I really missed them, However, we got back into a routine enjoying our work and we soon made a small network of friends. At first, everything was going well and every day felt like an extended honeymoon. One of our new friends called Tanya became close and it happened very quickly. We were introduced through a work friend and within a short time we saw each other every week.

Tanya was the life and soul of any party. Originally from the UK, but now based in Hong Kong. She was pretty and very sexy although, she never tried to be that way. She was bisexual and wasn't shy about it, she shocked me many times. She would do the most unexpected things at the drop of a hat.

One night we went to the party district in central Hong Kong called Wan Chai. We chose a bar called 'Stella' with a dance floor and a live DJ. All these clubs and bars are crazily busy every night, especially on the weekend with people spilling out onto the streets. Anyhow, on that night we were in Stella's and we got a corner couch. I went to the bar to get drinks, (which was a mission). It was like a human obstacle course and you needed to move with the bodies; up and down. It probably took about ten minutes to get the drinks!

As I was returning to the table, I saw Tanya and Lucy kissing. Tanya was on top of Lucy with both her hands on each side of Lucy's head. She had her tongue down her throat and was grinding Lucy with her body. I don't know what stopped me, but something did and it was one of those regrets I will always have. I just stood there watching angrily. I find it strange that I was more angry with Lucy than Tanya. I looked away and got back into the up and down movement of the crowd. I remember feeling so angry I wanted to smash something, anything and I threw the drinks against a wall and shouted,

"Fuck!" Luckily, no security saw me do it and it helped to sober me up. Then, I went back to the girls but they were gone from the corner. Eventually I found them by a speaker dancing. Not together, but in the same area,

"Katie! I've been looking for you everywhere!" Lucy shouted at me.

"Are you okay?" Tanya said searching my face as she said it. I gave them the okay sign and we started dancing together. I felt it best not to speak for a while and we didn't speak properly until we got home.

"I saw what happened tonight in the club Lucy with you and Tanya!"

"Oh, you mean Tanya forcing herself on me?"

"Is that what happened?"

"What do you bloody mean Katie? Did you think that was me doing the kissing?"

Lucy jumped up with this and looked really pissed off.

"All I saw was you two kissing on the couch Lucy! I was fuming and smashed our drinks. I didn't know what to think." I stood up and went to take her in my arms, but she pulled away and slapped me in the face. I saw red and we had our first fight. All I recall is slapping, throwing, rolling on top of each other and things being smashed in the process. It went on for ages and didn't help. Lucy was so angry and she couldn't control her emotions. I remember being very scared of her and it went on until there was a loud knock on the front door.

When Lucy opened the door the police were standing there; two male police officers. Lucy tried to push them away with her hands, not so strongly, but she pushed them both to close the door and shouted,

"Fuck off!" They didn't, instead Lucy was handcuffed and arrested. I begged them to stop but they were on a mission and they took her away leaving me in the flat. They told me,

"You don't say more. You not do more. She come with us. You stay here."

POLICE STATION

Lucy was taken away by the police that night to the Central police station. I was so stressed and didn't know what would happen, also, the flat was a mess from our fighting. The first thing I did was make a cup of tea and I sat there in the dark sipping my tea taking in the chaos. Then, I started cleaning up; it took about two hours and created two big bags of trash. My next concern was what to do about Lucy and I contemplated calling her dad. I changed my mind in the end, deciding to go to the police station in the morning.

After a restless night I arrived at the station at eight in the morning. Luckily, they spoke English at the front desk and asked me for my details, then I had to write a witness statement. The case was discussed with the officer in charge and he granted bail. He explained that the case had to go to a magistrates court for a judge to decide the penalty.

Lucy was eventually released by noon that morning and she looked terrible. The first thing she did was hug me and say sorry.

"I'm so sorry Katie, there is no excuse for my behaviour last night and I regret everything!" She said this through deep body shaking tears which set me off and I apologised too. We were given a court date for December sixth at ten in the morning and allowed to leave the station.

Making up is always good and that was what we did all day. I asked Lucy about what happened in the cells but she didn't want to talk about it. She did reassure me that nothing bad happened, only that they had given her breakfast and she was in a single cell. Lucy told me that Tanya had forced herself on her and what I had seen was not two ways. I apologised for jumping to conclusions and we moved on.

It was like a new beginning and we

promised to never let that kind of thing happen again. We also decided it would be best to tell Tanya that our friendship was over. I did it the easy way and sent her a message; I never got a reply.

December sixth came quickly. We went to the court in suits and Lucy's lawyer was sure it would only be a fine. She recommended that Lucy apologise to the officers at the first chance and explain that she was completely drunk. The lawyer also recommended saying that Lucy had a memory blank about the whole event.

Courts are depressing places filled with all sorts of people. There were worried family members, young guys trying to look cool and Lawyers running around looking busy. When we went in I had to sit at the back of the court and Lucy stood at the bench. The judge came in and everyone bowed. The two police officers were there too. Lucy did well I think and cried during her apology. The judge gave a fine for one thousand dollars and Lucy was told if she got in trouble through drinking again she would do time in prison.

We thanked the lawyer and left feeling lucky more than anything. We agreed the whole thing could of been worse and decided to not drink until christmas. I felt that time of no drinking brought us closer than ever before. Christmas was enjoyed with Lucy's family in their home. It was a great time and we both had a week of work. I love christmas and that was one of my favourites.

I bought Lucy a pair of Mikimoto pearl earrings for christmas and my funniest memory was the opening of the presents. It was a classic family time with the decorations up, carols playing in the background, lights flickering and it was in the morning. I went first and gave Lucy the small present looking forward to her reaction. Everybody was sat around the tree watching as Lucy peeled of the wrapping paper. I could see the delight on her face when she saw them, but then she started laughing. Her head went back and her deep loud laugh filled the room. I was confused. What was funny? Within a minute everybody except me was laughing.

"Here is your present Katie," and she passed a present the same size as the one I'd given here. I opened it to find a pair of Mikimoto pearl earrings staring at me and that made us all laugh again. Apparently, for Lucy it had been difficult to find a present for me and she had asked her family for advice.

We put the earrings on and were both very happy with our presents. Everyone got presents and enjoyed a wonderful time together. A great memory for me was playing cards in the afternoon. I told everyone about my luck at the casino and sure enough; I cleaned up. The day was completed by singing christmas carols around the piano played by David.

Lucy and I never told her family about the arrest or any friends. That felt the right decision and we slowly forgot all about it. Two thousand and eighteen was seen in with family and a big party at their home with about forty people. We also enjoyed drinking again but in moderation. We promised to make two thousand and eighteen a great year and decided to try Thailand out for living on our honeymoon.

THAILAND

When the time came to go to Thailand we were more than ready. We had been living a very quiet life since the arrest and were ready for adventure. We bought tickets to Bangkok and got our visas. Our plan was simple; stay in Bangkok for a week then go south to the islands.

Bangkok is a beautiful and exciting city. The wildest city we had ever seen and from the minute we arrived things got crazy. The first shock was the heat; it was like stepping into a furnace and then there's the noise. We booked a youth hostel in the city centre and all around us was noise. Traffic was the loudest with motorbikes rushing everywhere, sometimes with three people on one scooter or carrying an unbelievable load. The streets were noisy with people, music and the street stall workers with their shouting.

Shopping in Thailand is a new experience. The stall owners shout at you, pull and push you to buy their goods, but before you buy anything you had better be ready to barter.

"Hey lady, you like these T-shirts? Very cheap, only five dollars. Look, look! This is your size, please try!" Then they were sizing the T-shirts on us and we bought five T-shirts in the end for twenty dollars. This was on our way to the youth hostel, they were very convincing.

Eventually, we found our youth hostel and it was a dump. Paper thin, dirty walls with grotty shared toilets and showers. The only good thing was the lounge area where we met lots of backpackers full of fun stories, Bangkok is a hub for backpackers traveling around Asia. One guy from New Zealand invited us out that night and we accepted. It was his last night in Thailand and he wanted to enjoy it. His name was Jack and he'd been travelling for three months. He said he could show us the sights of Bangkok on a budget and we liked him immediately. He didn't look like your typical backpacker because he wore designer clothes, was clean shaven and had a suitcase.

We met him after showering outside the youth hostel and together jumped into a "TukTuk". These are the way to see Bangkok; they look like a motorbike with an open sided chariot on the back. The driver was very friendly and Jack told him where he wanted to go.

"When you ride these things ladies be sure to fix the price first with the driver, otherwise you'll be charged an arm and a bloody leg." Then Jack negotiated with the driver and it took about five minutes.

We enjoyed the sights and stopped a few times. The floating market was first which was very colourful, then a large Golden temple, a beautiful park and an infamous place called "Pa-Pong".

Pa-Pong is the red light district of Bangkok with three streets full of bars, clubs, prostitutes and shows. There are also lots of "Ladyboys". They are often stunning, very bold and sometimes you can't tell if they are a ladyboy or a real women. We went to a ladyboy show and they loved us straightaway. That was when Jack found out we were a couple, but he didn't care and once that was cleared up he told us that the reason for his traveling was due to splitting up with his boyfriend in NZ.

It felt good to be completely open about our love and know he understood us. Sometimes, I felt uncomfortable being open, so that was very refreshing, it was also easy to do in Thailand as amost everything is excepted there.

All of us went to a sex show next that I will never forget; the club was dark with a centre stage and what happened in two hours shocked me. I had heard about the clubs and the stories were true, I also felt sorry for the girls. I couldn't help feeling it was all faked and forced. There is a dark side to that kind of entertainment and I was glad to leave the club at the end of the show.

Next was a local bar where the locals

made us welcome. We played pool and had a lot of fun playing for drinks but lost every game. We also experienced a fight which got very ugly. Some young drunk western lads thought it would be fun to harrass the ladyboys. Within seconds they were surrounded by angry ladyboys who attacked using heels and glass bottles. The guys didn't stand a chance and left bleeding and limping with their tails between their legs.

By the morning we were drunk and exhausted. It was a night to remember and all on a budget. Jack had to leave in the morning to fly home and we promised to keep in touch. We stayed in Bangkok for six more nights and every night was a party. We enjoyed a Thai massage everyday and sightseeing, then drinking with the locals at night. One morning Lucy was having a facial massage. I had popped out to buy a drink and when I came back she was sat in a reclined chair with her eyes closed and the lady was behind her giving her a facial. I slipped in and gestured for her to be quiet and let me take over. I started gently and slowly built up the massage. By the time Lucy realised something wasn't right, I was slapping her forehead hard. She opened her eyes and saw me smiling at her. That was a good memory, although I had to pay for the massage. After the six days it was time for the islands and we bought train tickets for an island called Koh Samui.

The train was overnight and very cheap. For most of the journey we enjoyed playing cards with some Thai men and sharing their food. Thai food is often very spicy, but so tasty. We were also able buy food and drinks to share with them when we stopped in the train stations. People would come up to the window selling all sorts of wierd and wonderful goods.

Koh Samui island is paradise with golden sand beaches and the ocean is very beautiful. It's a small Island blessed with palm trees, jungles and lots of partying. I think that's why most people go there; to party. Every night of the week the bars were packed with people who want to have fun. There are people from all over the world with lots of good music, drink and drugs.

On our second night Lucy tricked me

into taking magic mushrooms in a shake. Lucy told me it was a local popular cocktail and I believed her. That night was the most messed up we'd ever been. They start working after about thirty minutes and the first thing I noticed was everything became like bright disco colours. Every movement was exaggerated and my body became so relaxed with traces from movement everywhere. I had trouble talking at some points and Lucy was wild. My memories of that night are broken and there are gaps, but I remember the deep laughter was non stop and the need to vomit.

We went from bar to bar and I hate to think what we looked like. Somehow we were like magnets and picked different characters up on the way. At one point, we found ourselves at a beach party and I remember dancing like I'd never danced before, everything felt perfect with smiling people, good tunes and the warm sea breeze. We swam in our clothes, rolled in the sand and got cuts and bruises from nowhere. At one point I remember Lucy innocently asking me,

"Where am I?" I laughed and then realised she was being serious.

"We are in heaven!" Was my mumbled reply. That was one of my last memories before waking up in a little wooden hut by myself feeling close to death.

The hut belonged to the owner of the land who had ten huts and a little restaurant. His name was Charlie and he appeared once I stumbled out of the hut in the morning.

"Good morning Princess! How you feeling?" I could just about move and talking was almost impossible but I managed to ask him,

"Have you seen my friend? Her name is Lucy."

"She's on the beach over there, we put you in the hut because you fell asleep on the beach. I had to carry you."

"Really…ummmm, I'm so sorry!"

"Not a problem, come on let's join your friends!" He led the way to the beach and soon I found Lucy with a few others. She was still dancing, but there was no more music. When she saw me she looked so happy in a mad way. No shoes, hair all over the place and her eyes were the biggest I've ever seen them. There was dried blood all over her dress too.

"Katie! Are you okay? Did you sleep? Are you hungry? Where did you go?" She said all this so fast. I was happy to see her but instantly worried about her.

"I'm okay Lucy, I think I need a coffee." We went to the restaurant and had coffee until Lucy started to talk nonsense at the table and offending other guests. Charlie kindly offered for us to use the same hut and I gladly accepted his offer. That was the wildest love making ever for us and we spent the day in that little hut recovering and loving. It was a big comedown and we were in there for about twenty hours.

Charlie was a nice guy and we stayed at his place for the rest of our trip. It was a wild time and we had a lot of fun, we went scuba diving, go-karting and made lots of friends. But strangely, by the end of our trip, we felt it was time to move on. Thailand is a great country, but we didn't think it would be good for our health or our relationship. Hong Kong was calling and we decided to go home.

BACK HOME

We arrived in Hong Kong on the twentieth of January in two thousand and eighteen. It felt really good to be back home with our own bed, a wardrobe of clothes, and all the things that made it home. Also, we had four days until starting work. Our jobs in the international kindergarten were fun, challenging and rewarding, but hard work.

"Well Katie, here we are back home, it's been so much fun. The wedding was wonderful, our families have bonded, accepted our marriage, and what's more I love you more everyday!"

"I love you too and I'm starving, I could eat a horse, we need to go shopping!"

"Okay, I'll go now and get some goodies. See you in half an hour chubby cheeks!" I grabbed our recyclable shopping bag, my purse and hit the streets.

Shopping in Hong Kong is an adventure for me as I always find things never tried and the supermarkets are full of interesting people. I often meet people and hear their different stories. They are usually the older generation and their stories are often funny or sometimes sad. That day I met a Chinese man in his sixties, he was wearing a worn suit and it matched his worn, tired looking face. He told me about how good life used to be in Hong Kong.

"Are you English?"

"No, I'm from Australia."

"You look like an English lady. I like English and uhmm… they were good for us. I had a textile business shipping all over the world, but now I have nothing. Since the English left things are not good."

"I'm sorry to hear that. I love Hong Kong and it's my new home."

"I love Hong Kong too…uhmm, but life is

hard now. Work hard lady and save money. You might need savings one day! Have a nice day." Then he was gone. I bought lots of food and found some new treats. I wasn't sure what they were but they looked like mini savoury pies.

By the time I got home Lucy was already in a party mood with music playing and a bottle of red had been started.

"Hi Katie! You'd better get ready cause we are meeting my brothers soon." This was a classic Lucy surprise. Our original plan was to eat together at home, then go to Zinni's. But I liked the idea of meeting her brothers so went with the new plan. It didn't take long to get ready and it was a beautiful night with clear skies and a perfect temperature. I found out we were still going to Zinni's and were meeting her brothers in the club at nine.

Dinner was eaten at home and the pies were delicious, then we caught the tram and enjoyed seeing the sights of Hong Kong again. The city was always interesting to live in and I never grew tired of it.

Full of action with all sorts of people and cultures. It's such a mix of old and new, east and west, plus it's own uniqueness. This also describes Zinni's. It's a big old club famous for having over forty variations of gin cocktails, people from all walks of life and good music. It's in an old workshop with a really modern interior. We met her brothers in the club and it was packed. We all tried different gins that were very tasty and it wasn't long before we were on the dance floor. That was when I saw Tanya, she came straight up to me with fire in her eyes.

"Well look who's out tonight; miss jealous! Are you still jealous?"

"No, I'm miss fucking angry! Angry with you, what you did was out of line. You knew me and Lucy are a couple."

"Yes, I did, but she's irresistible! By the way, you look very sexy tonight Katie!" Then she smiled and tried to kiss me, so I pushed her back, turned away and went looking for Lucy. I found her in conversation with her brothers.

"Watch out tonight Lucy because that bitch Tanya is here."

"Oh god, that's all we need. How about I go and tell her to piss off?"

"I don't think that's a good idea, let's just stay away from her." I wondered if it was possible. Lucy's brothers wanted to know what we were talking about, so Lucy explained there was an unwanted friend in the club. David came to the rescue with,

"Don't you worry ladies. You've got protection tonight, come on, let's dance." I don't know what happened to Tanya, but we never saw her again that night and we left the club at two in the morning. Lucy's brother David invited us to his place for a night cap and he took us there in a taxi.

David had style; you could see it in his fashion sense and in his home. Very simple, but classy, practical and stylish. It was originally a workshop that had been converted creating a big living area with an island kitchen. It was a big space with large windows and concrete walls. He had three large sofas and we made ourselves comfy. David put on some jazz, opened a bottle of champagne and he asked Lucy,

"So, how was your honeymoon?"

"We enjoyed crazy Bangkok first, then we went to a lovely little island called Koh Samui. We probably partied too much and spent more money than expected, but hey, it was our honeymoon after all." She was obviously drunk but still able to converse.

"I've heard Bangkok is crazy, did you have any problems there?" Tom asked me this in a caring way.

"No problems for us. The hostel was a bit rough in Bangkok, but it's a beautiful and exciting city. There is so much to do and see. We met a lot of interesting people too. It's a hub for travelers in Asia." I wanted to tell them about the seedy side, but decided to stop there. Then Lucy took over,

"We watched a couple of sex shows and saw women doing things I'd never even heard about. They used ping pong balls, then razor blades and finally a bottle of coke! It was unbelievable and I felt sorry for the women. Unfortunately, slavery still exists in some countries."

"How about you two, what are your plans?" Tom said this to me. He was a very handsome guy and I felt very comfortable with him.

"Back to work in a couple of days and enjoying life back in Hong Kong. Other than that, we've talked about moving to Australia for a change. Nothing decided, but the more I think about it, the more I like the idea." I said this looking at Lucy. She was with us again and gave me a big smile.

"Let's do it Katie, how about saving for about six months, then try our luck down under?" My simple answer was,

"Okay," We ended up all sleeping at David's place that night and it was a memorable night, then in the morning we all went to a popular cafe called Mamas.

Mamas was big, noisy and very friendly.

You have to share a round table with others usually and for me that's part of the fun. Everyone helps with ordering food and this is done by ticking Chinese characters on a sheet of paper. The food is then brought to you on a tray. There are also people walking around with food trolleys and you can take food of them as you like. We had dim sum, pastries, fried fish and sponge cake. You can also drink as much Chinese tea as you like. That morning we met a young couple on our table and they helped us to order.

They thought David was Nicholas Cage, so we played along with it and they even took photos of us all together. I pretended to be his wife, Tom his brother and Lucy his bossy manager. Lucy pretended to be angry about David eating too much and told everyone he was training for his next movie, so he had to follow a strict diet. They sympathized with her and told him to listen to Lucy. This attracted the attention of others and David became very popular. It was so funny and harmless and when we finally left, everybody was waving and asking for signatures.

The first day at work went well and everyone wanted to know about our honeymoon in Thailand. We didn't give all the details; skipping the parts which were inappropriate. The students were an average age of four and very cute. We played lots of games and sung some songs. I loved that job and the children always gave me power. The weeks went fast and life was good for both of us. That was until a phone call from my parents.

My best friend Helen had been involved in a car accident and was hurt badly. Apparently, she had gone into the back of a truck and was crushed in her seat. She was on a life support machine and had asked for me. It's amazing how one minute everything is going well then, boom your world comes crashing down.

I got the call at work and my manager said I had to go and that they could cover my classes.

NSW

New South Wales is a beautiful part of the world full of deep green lush nature. That was the first thing I noticed driving from the airport to my parent's house in my rented car. I hadn't been there for a few years and it felt good to be back. Everything looked fresh, full of life and it was summer, my favorite season. After living in big cities it was good to be in the countryside again. My plan was to go to my parent's home first then straight to the hospital to see Helen.

Me and Helen had been friends since primary school and I loved her so much. She was my best friend and I prayed for the first time in years whilst driving, (with my eyes open).

"God, ermm, it's me Katie. I want to ask a big favor. I know I haven't checked in with you for a long time, but we need your help more than ever. Can you please help Helen to pull through this. She's a good person and deserves a good life, if anyone can help it's you. In the name of our lord Jesus Christ I pray Amen."

It felt the right thing to do and I realized I was crying silent tears which I could feel rolling down my face. I also had a strong tingling sensation all over my body, it was the same feeling I often get when I say hello to strangers. I can't explain it well, but it's a good feeling and very human, some emotions are not easy to express in words. I wiped away the tears and turned into my parent's drive.

As soon as I switched off the engine my parents were at the front door coming to greet me. We hugged strongly and there was no need for words. Everybody was crying and it was a mixture of relief, despair and love. We had last seen each other a few months ago when they visited us in Hong Kong for the wedding and that was the last time I'd seen Helen.

"What's the update on Helen Mum?"

"She's in and out of consciousness and in intensive care. We were there yesterday and her family is by her bedside night and day. They are such lovely people and keeping strong."

"Why don't we go now?" Dad said this and guided us to his Jeep.

We got to the hospital in thirty minutes and once directed to the correct wing we met her parents. I'd never seen them looking so unkempt and tired; it was as if they had suddenly aged. Helen's mum Heather gave us the latest news.

"She keeps slipping in and out of consciousness and will be going in for surgery today hopefully. Her lungs are lacerated and she has both internal and external bleeding of the lungs."

"Oh, my God, can I see her now?" I asked this through tears and at that moment all I wanted to do was hold her hand and tell Helen everything would be okay. The doctor arrived and introductions were made. She said I could go in and at present Helen was conscious.

Nothing could of prepared me for what I first saw. Helen was in bed surrounded by tubes and machines. She was looking at me through her bandages and all I could see were her bruised, bloodshot eyes.

She was trying to speak so I put my ear to her mouth and heard,

"Thank you." I completely broke down and held her hand for a long time physically shaking with the deep crying.

"Sorry Katie, no seatbelt."

"Don't worry Helen, everything will be fine. Keep positive and soon you will be home." We only had about ten minutes together before they asked me to leave, then we watched her being wheeled into surgery and said goodbye at the operating room doors.

Those were the longest five hours of my life. Conversation was difficult and didn't help, I didn't know what to say and spent most of the time looking at the floor.

Finally, the doctor came to us and immediately I knew it was not good as she approached Helen's parents,

"I'm so sorry to tell you this, but we lost Helen during surgery. We did our best and so did she, her injuries were to severe."

This caused everyone to lose self control and there were no words, just a pouring out of loss, anger and pain. The doctor patiently waited, then informed us that we could see Helen in an hour to say goodbye.

When you see a loved one who has passed away it's very painful and I kept hoping she would open her eyes and smile at me. I tried to control my emotions but that was impossible. I cried the most I ever have in my life holding her cold hands.

They say time is a great healer but it can take a long time sometimes to work. At first, I found myself walking the streets in the middle of the night. I felt angry, miserable and I stopped eating properly. I couldn't sleep for more than three hours and all I could think about was Helen. Sometimes I would find myself laughing out loud at a certain memory and other times crying into my pillow. I spoke to Lucy everyday on Skype and missed her more than ever. My family we're obviously worried about me and gave me good support.

The funeral was heartbreaking. Helen's family and friends came and we said our final farewells. When you lose someone so young it is very depressing and hard to accept.

Things started getting better for me after a while and I began to accept the loss of my best friend. Slowly my thoughts focused on the future. My mum helped a lot to make that happen and I remember her saying,

"You can't go on like this Katie. Helen wouldn't want it for sure; she'd want to see you back to your old self. You only have one life on earth so make it count. Lucy needs you and we need you." That was a good wake up call and I started planning my next steps.

I also began to look at my hometown through new eyes and appreciated my family and friends more than ever. It was after a day of soul searching and weighing up the pros and cons of what to do; that I decided to ask Lucy if she would join me in Australia to live. I was sure if we both got work it would all be fine and I felt Sydney would be a good place to live. That evening I called Lucy as usual on Skype and told her my thoughts.

"Lucy, can you come here? Let's live here together for a while. If it doesn't work out we can go back to Hong Kong." Lucy's reply surprised me.

"I thought you'd never ask, I'd love to come. In fact, I've already spoken to the school and my family about it. The school wants one months notice to find another teacher and my family think it's a good idea coming to Australia. I'll be there in April for your birthday."

"That's fantastic! How about we stay with my parents for a bit, then move to Sydney. You'll love Sydney and we should be able to get you a spousal visa too."

"Right, I'll go to the Embassy tomorrow and get the ball rolling, I'm excited already. Love you!"

I told my parents and they were happy to hear the news. My father said he could get us some local work on a farm if we wanted it. He had a friend called Jack who had a farm and needed workers. I was sure the fresh air and labour would be a nice change and we could save money.

HOMETOWN

My hometown is a pretty place, very friendly and surrounded by nature. I was feeling a lot better about life and enjoying living there. Everything felt familiar but somehow smaller. I had built a ritual of waking up at seven, then a long shower followed by having breakfast with mum, then going for a walk. My walks varied, but always involved a visit to Helen's grave where I often met her dad. He brought fresh flowers everyday and we enjoyed reminiscing about Helen.

Dad took me to the farm his friend owned to meet Jack. He was a very jovial man and I liked him instantly. He needed shop assistants for selling groceries, packers and pickers. I took a job as a shop assistant and he convinced me to start the next day, he also guaranteed Lucy a job.

My day on the farm started at eight in the morning and finished at five. I was working with two other ladies Angel and Barbara. Angel was Jack's niece and a pleasure to work with; not the smartest but so positive and friendly. She was only eighteen and full of teenage stories of boyfriends, parties and horses. She rode her horse everyday and after meeting her horse, I had a new friend too. What a beauty and I was surprised how much I liked the horse, she was muscular and very intelligent. The first time I rode her was after work, it wasn't my first time and I was nervous, however after about thirty minutes I was having the time of my life.

Barbara was in her forties and a mother of two. She had been working in the shop for a long time and helped me learn the ropes.

First I had to make sure we were ready to open and display the fruits and vegetables which I enjoyed doing very much. I took pride in my work and was very satisfied once I'd displayed and priced everything. Jack praised my work and I noticed the job was helping to heal me. I was sleeping better, eating well and feeling happier, also my birthday was coming and so was Lucy.

My birthday is on the fifth of April and Lucy was arriving in three days on the second. The plan was to pick Lucy up from the airport in Sydney and stay in a hotel the first night. I'd found a hotel near the airport and had booked a double room. It wasn't as private as a Japanese love hotel, but in Australia, same-sex marriage was becoming more and more acceptable. Just this year same-sex marriage had been legalised. As for my birthday, my parents wanted to have a home party. I had said yes and was looking forward to my birthday party. This hadn't happened since I was a little girl; now I was nearly twenty seven.

I got the day off work to pick up Lucy and the day soon came. I got the train to Sydney airport and waited eagerly for Lucy. Suddenly I felt a tap on my shoulder and was pulled from my daydreaming by Lucy. She looked amazing and we were so happy to see each other. We embraced and had a long kiss; it was a kiss worth a thousand words.

"Welcome to Australia Lucy, I'm sure you're going to love it here. It's so good to see you again!"

"You too Katie, I've missed you more than you know, skyping was nice but there's definitely limits. Shall we go to the hotel now cause I'm dying to get you naked."

"That's the plan! We'll be there in about an hour. How was your flight?"

"The usual, a few movies, shit food and too long in one seat. All I have wanted for ages is to be with you again."

"The feelings mutual chubby cheeks, so come on let's get going." We caught a taxi to our hotel called The Bay Hotel.

Our hotel was situated on Sydney harbour and our room had an amazing view of the bay. Lucy wanted to freshen up, so we took a shower together. We washed each other and enjoyed a slow romantic shower time. Everything felt new and exciting, Lucy felt new and making love was like the first time all over again, except we knew each other better and knew what turned the other on, we were both loving, gentle and slow. We also talked and laughed constantly; except when talking about Helen, that made us both cry.

The sun started setting and we enjoyed watching the sunset naked with a bottle of red wine, the harbour view and relaxed conversation. I will never forget that night, I felt so lucky to be alive and with the one I loved, I'm sure that losing a loved one makes you appreciate what you have more. I was also confident things would go well for us in Australia. I told her more about the job she was to start next week and the people she would be working with.

"I like the farm job more than teaching, it's less stress and very healthy. The people are great and the money's not bad, by the way, have you ever ridden a horse?"

"A long time ago, I'd like to try again. Also, I was wondering, how long until we move to Sydney Katie?"

"I guess about three months should do. We don't need to pay any rent and life is simple in my hometown, why don't we go out tonight in Sydney for dinner while we are here?"

"And drinks darling, I want to party tonight. Sounds good?" Actually, it didn't, all I wanted to do was relax and catch up with Lucy. But I hid my true feelings, smiled and agreed.

We had another shower, got dressed and decided to start in the 'Rocks'. This part of Sydney is very trendy and is next to the harbour. After a walk along the promenade we found an Italian restaurant that looked and smelled very inviting. I had my favourite Italian dish carbonara and Lucy had meat sauce pasta. We shared everything, plus a salad and a bottle of red wine. We fed each other food and played footsie under the table. It was a lovely meal and we enjoyed catching up. Once we'd finished the wine I was getting in a party mood.

We went to Kings Cross which is the party capital of Sydney with an interesting mix of rough and classy. We went to a 'Live house' club that was busy and funky. There was a band playing some rock music and the atmosphere was lively, some were dancing, others talking. It wasn't too loud and the club was big. Within ten minutes Lucy was in deep conversation with a group of ladies. This happened whilst I was at the bar getting drinks. As I approached, Lucy pointed me out and the four ladies waved. When I finally got to them, introductions were made.

They were a local rock group and they looked a wild bunch. The vocalist was Liz with spiked purple hair and her partner was Marge the drummer. Marge had a shaved head and piercings everywhere. The keyboardist was big Jacqui and the guitarist was Shelly. Their band was called 'The Licks' and they invited us to come see them play on April fifth; my birthday. I tried to explain we already had plans but Lucy looked at me all excited.

"Why don't we try to change your party

venue? It would be a great birthday and I'm sure your family would love it too!" I didn't know what to say, it might work, everything depended on my family.

"Why don't I call my mum and ask?" Everyone agreed that was a good idea so I left the bar and called Mum.

"Hi Mum, we've been invited to see a rock band play in Sydney. The only problem is the date, it's on my birthday this Thursday. Do you mind if we change the venue and have the party in a big club with live music? I think it will be easier for you."

"Sure Katie, it's your party. I'll let everyone know tomorrow, just send me a link to the place and the time. How's Lucy?"

"Great! It's so nice to have her here and thank you Mum, you rock!"

"Sounds like I will on Thursday. Have a good time and looking forward to seeing you both."

I went back in and told them the good

news. I sent a link to Mum and then we all had a dance together. It turned out to be a great night, the group were nice people and we had a good time together. At midnight we made our way home after saying goodbye. We didn't sleep much that night because we stayed up talking and catching up, it was a very special time. I was so happy to be with Lucy again and realised more than ever how much she meant to me.

Thursday night soon came and we all went to the club together. My parents had told everyone to dress for a rock party.

Mum and Dad looked really cool with denim outfits and white T-shirts. Dad had spiked his grey hair and looked ten years younger. Other family members and friends met us outside the club and we were ready to party.

Once inside we met 'The Licks' and enjoyed drinking and talking together before their set. They had also made an area for us in the club with balloons and a big sign saying, 'HAPPY BIRTHDAY KATIE.' After about an hour a cake was brought out and a buffet. Everyone in the club sang happy birthday to me which made me cry. I also got some presents, a dress from my parents and a perfume from Lucy. Someone from my family started calling,

"Speech, speech," and I was given a mike.

"Thank you everybody for coming. I am now twenty seven, young enough to party, but old enough to know my limits. So I'm going home now!" This made everybody laugh.

"That's about all I want to say except, a big thank you to my family and friends and my wife Lucy, I love you all. I think it's time for 'The Licks' to play so my birthday wish is that we all dance together." And that is what happened. The Licks were really good and everyone said it was a fantastic night. We all stayed until one in the morning then went our seperate ways. It truly was the best birthday party ever for me.

TENGOKU

After my birthday party we enjoyed the weekend at my parent's home and we all got on so well. In fact, it was such a wonderful time that Lucy called it 'Tengoku' which means heaven in Japanese.

Sunday we all went horse riding on the farm where I introduced Lucy to Jack and Angel. Jack showed Lucy around and Angel gave us horse riding lessons. It was forecast to rain, but we got lucky and managed to ride in between light showers. Lucy was so comical on a horse, very tense and bouncing around on the horse like a puppet. She was in pain afterwards and needed to have a rest.

Dad did a BBQ and as always it was amazing, he's a BBQ master and gets satisfaction from watching people enjoy his cooking, not only the wonderful variety of seafoods and meats, but homemade sauces and salads too. Lucy was the life and soul of any party and that weekend was no different. She updated us about her family and life in Hong Kong. Her parents were taking a cruise in the Caribbean and in good health. They had also promised a visit once we were ready for guests. Her brothers seemed busy working and Tom was in love again, apparently he was thinking of getting engaged this year if she said yes.

It made me happy watching my parents interact so well and naturally with Lucy. We spoke about Helen and agreed she must be in 'Tengoku'. Life is cruel and unfair sometimes, to take someone so young just didn't make sense. I always wear my seatbelt now and make sure others do; life is too precious to lose over such a small detail. I will never forget Helen and still miss her very much.

Monday was Lucy's first day at work and she was both hardworking and popular. We spent the morning in the shop and worked well together. She was going to experience two hours at each different job as a kind of orientation. She made conversation with the customers easily and received many compliments about her looks. I watched her have an interesting conversation with a regular highly opinionated old lady.

"What do you think of Donald Trump young lady?"

"Well, he's good at following through on his promises, but I wonder how good he is at everything else. Also, some of his promises are very debatable. Will a wall between Mexico and America change anything?"

"Yes, it will stop illegal immigrants getting into the US."

"Maybe, but I think it is bad for relationships between the two countries. Did you know the stats say he's told more than three thousand lies so far?"

"Really? What about Brexit. Do you think that is a good idea?"

"Yes and no. It's very complicated at the moment and I feel sorry for Theresa May. To please everybody is impossible and I hope she gets more support to get the job done. I think they will leave but with no deal."

"That's not good for Britian is it. I hope they make a deal soon. Nice talking to you young lady and I look forward to seeing you next week." Lucy looked at me once she was gone and blew her cheeks out.

"Bit early for that! Is she always that intense?" Barbara started laughing and told us that the old lady loved chatting and sometimes stayed in the shop for an hour if they weren't busy.

We didn't show affection or tell anyone we were married that morning, but at lunchtime I broached the subject.

"Do you feel comfortable telling people we are married Lucy?"

"Yes and no. I think it would be easiest not to say anything, but it doesn't feel right. We should be able to be who we are anywhere, if showing affection to the people you love in public is a problem, then that issue needs addressing immediately, I think we shouldn't hide anything. In fact, once we are settled I want us to become parents." This last sentence caught me off guard.

"Really, do you mean adopt or artificial insemination? You know how to keep me on my toes Lucy! Obviously, I've thought about this before and think it would be wonderful."

"Adopting suits us best I think Katie; we can help someone less fortunate and make our family. I've been looking into adopting and it's a lot easier here in Australia than Hong Kong."

"Tell me more!" I knew it wouldn't be simple and definitely one of the biggest decisions in my life.

"Since two thousand and ten it has been legal in New South Wales for same-sex married couples to adopt and since last year the whole country. Because we are married it will be easier and they will want to know we are suitable parents. We need to show we can provide financially and their main concern as is ours is for the well being of the child. If we meet the criteria, adopting can be domestic or from overseas, personally, I like the idea of domestic adoption. I would also like to adopt a child with special needs; we could really help them I think."

"Wow Lucy, you really have been looking into this, it's difficult for me to say right now, but I guess domestic would save language issues and probably easier than international. My first thought is we need to have secure jobs and a home, we don't have either yet!"

"That's true, but if we stick to your original plan of going to Sydney in July, getting a home with a spare room and getting good jobs, we might be able to start this by the end of the year."

"Okay, let's start saving from now for our new home and start job hunting in Sydney, what kind of work do you want to do Lucy?"

"I studied international management in university and would like to use that if possible, and you?"

"One of my old school friends works in sales and marketing in Sydney; if she can help me get in, I'll take it. The last time we spoke, she said it was fun work and good money, she also said they needed people in her company and asked if I was interested. I'll send her a message now."

"That sounds like the way to go Katie! I'm going to look at job agencies tonight after work."

Lucy did well on her first day and after watching her work, I knew she would be fine anywhere. I saw a different side to her in the workplace, serious, passionate and a good listener. I sent a message to my friend Jane and got a reply ten minutes later. The message said she'd recommend me highly and to send my resume; also that they needed someone ASAP. As for Lucy, she was surprised how many jobs were available in her line of work. We read each ad and found two we thought sounded promising, a Human Resources officer and a position in international business development.

We worked on our resumes together after work and thought they looked good after about three hours. We wrote cover letters and triple checked them; then sent everything by email. I remember how excited I was.

That night I had trouble sleeping, I kept thinking of living and working in Sydney. Could we adopt if we were both working? Could Lucy calm down? Many things didn't add up yet, so I decided to write it all down to help get my head around everything. This is what I wrote,
Find a home with a spare room
Get jobs
Good and bad points of adoption
Apply for Lucy's permanent resident visa

I wrote this in order of priority, but was still uncertain about many points. When I have major decisions, I write the pros and cons of all the different scenarios to see which one wins the most points and adopting won the most points compared to not adopting. Helping a child who needs it felt a good choice.

I finally fell asleep and dreamed of our happy life as a family. In my dream we had a fantastic apartment on the harbour and money wasn't an issue. We had three beautiful children and they were the joy of our lives. Together we did everything in the dream and I remember the love I felt for them was heart wrenching and powerful. Most of the dream seemed to be based in parks and on the beaches in Sydney. At the end of the dream they were grown up and looking after us. The tables had turned with me and Lucy being fed by them and wheeled around town in wheelchairs. Lucy had aged well and we still loved each other strongly.

The first thing I did in the morning was check for a reply and was disappointed that there was nothing. Lucy reminded me it was seven in the morning and no one was in the office yet, so I decided to forget about it and focus on the farm job. Lucy was placed in packaging and we only met once in the day for lunch.

"Hi Lucy, how's it going in packaging?"

"It's alright, but to be honest with you, my mind has been elsewhere all morning. I hope we get interviews soon, a big apartment and a child to make us a family of three."

"That's a lot to ask for Lucy, but I like your style, fingers crossed our dreams will come true!"

When we got home we sat together at the desktop computer, Lucy went first and was pleased to see an email.

It was from a company called Allergeen and they needed a HR officer. They were interested in meeting Lucy at her convenience, so she gave them some available dates and sent her reply. We were both elated at this, then it was my turn. I also had a reply and an invitation to an interview, I gave some dates and sent my reply.

It was a good feeling to be potentially wanted in work with a future career and hopefully good money. I told my family who were happy to hear the update and wished us luck. We had a little celebration that night and even practiced interview questions we thought might be difficult, I went first,

"Why do you think we should employ you?" Lucy thought for a few seconds and replied,

"I can promise you that I will do my very best to not only be a good employee, but to help your company grow. I'm reliable, hardworking, take my job seriously and I work well in a team or individually. What I lack in experience I can make up for in passion."

"Nice answer Lucy."

"Your turn now Katie, what is your weak point?"

"People often say that I'm too positive. I know this is true, so I also try to be realistic. I believe this combination is good for both me and whoever I work for. I can help get through negativity and usually find a realistic solution to problems. Actually, in my last evaluation in the kindergarten, the president said I was too positive. I asked her if she'd like me to be more negative and the answer was no which became a joke between us."

Lucy liked that reply and offered me a job.

I got a reply first and they asked me to come to Sydney for an interview next week on the twelfth of April. Next was Lucy and coincidentally on the same day she had an interview in Sydney. We spent the week before the interviews practicing for them and went out to buy new suits. We went to Sydney a day early and stayed in a hotel, we also decided to let the girls from 'The Licks' know we were in town. They were free that evening and we made plans to meet after the interviews.

THE INTERVIEW

I got to the office ten minutes before the interview and my friend Jane was waiting for me in the reception. I hadn't seen her for a long time and really enjoyed seeing her again. We had been close in high school ten years ago and it was as if nothing had changed between us.

We'd been texting a lot over the last few days and I knew I was meeting her boss Mr Fuchino. I was nervous, confident and excited all at the same time. Jane wished me luck then led the way to his office, and left me there to knock on the door.

I was invited in and was greeted by three serious looking people. They asked me to sit down and the questions started. All was going well until at the end Mr Fuchino asked me,

"I heard you recently got married; congratulations. Is your husband happy about moving to Sydney?" The word 'husband' stumped me for a moment, then I realised Jane hadn't told them the whole story.

"I did get married last year in December to the love of my life. My wife's name is Lucy and to answer your question, she too is job hunting in Sydney and we hope to find jobs, then settle down long term. We both love Sydney and want to make it our home." I gave them my best smile and they all semi-smiled back.

"Thank you for your honesty and I like to think, we are an open minded company. This brings us to the end of the interview. Let me and my team have a quick meeting outside, we'll be back in about three minutes, is that okay with you?"

This was from one of the bosses called Ms Smart.

"That's fine with me." They left and it felt like ten minutes until they came back in and Mr Fuchino spoke first,

"Firstly, thank you for coming today and after talking to my colleagues, we would like to offer you a position in international sales. There will be a probation period of one month and after that, if both parties are happy we will give you a contract. Are you interested?"

"Yes, I am. And that sounds wonderful, thank you very much, I'm so pleased, and I promise to do my best for you." I was over the moon and floated out of the room. Jane was waiting for me and she only had to look at me to see what had happened.

"I knew they'd hire you Katie. You're gonna love it here and it's a great company. Don't get me wrong, it's hard sometimes but worth it." I thanked her and gave her a kiss. As soon as I got outside I called Lucy and she answered immediately.

"Hi Lucy, how did it go?"

"Hi you, I got the job and they want me to start as soon as possible. They also have an empty two bedroom apartment in Sydney we can use."

"Fantastic! I got the job too and they seemed really nice. I'm going to be doing international sales, how about you?"

"HR baby, this is going to jump start my career and yours. I'm so happy. Let's meet in Kings Cross and celebrate!"

"I'm on my way, see you in about twenty minutes."

I felt high, what a great day for both of us and everything was coming together. We had new jobs with a future and an apartment with a spare room. My next wish was that our jobs would go well and we could adopt. When I arrived at the club Lucy was already outside waiting. She ran to me and spun me around.

"The company looks good Katie and I will have a weeks training with the Lady I'm replacing. She was in the interview and we got on well. Her name's Tina and she seemed both kind and very experienced."

"I'm so pleased for you and that's great news about the apartment too! When can we move in?"

"I pick up the keys next week and start work in two weeks on Monday the thirtieth. I hope the farm will be okay with such a sudden change?"

"Leave that with me, Jack is a family friend, so there shouldn't be an issue, anyway, let's go inside and have a drink." We went in and the band met us, they were very happy to hear our news about getting jobs. Lucy bought a round of tequila shots which was the beginning of a wild night. I don't remember getting back to the hotel, but I do remember waking up in my clothes with a major hangover. Lucy wasn't much better and we spent the morning recovering. She made me laugh by saying,

"I'm never drinking tequila again Katie. In fact, my drinking days are over."

"I'd like a dollar for everytime I've heard you say that Lucy!"

In the evening we went back home, told

my family the big news and my dad kindly offered to call Jack. After the call he said Jack was happy for us and we could finish up whenever was best for us. We decided to work up to the twenty sixth and were given a farewell party on the farm. We had only been there a short time, but bonds were made and everybody promised to keep in touch. Jack also said if it didn't work out in Sydney we could work for him anytime.

They were some of the nicest people I'd ever worked with, honest, fun and very kind. It was easy to make good friendships in the countryside compared to a city. People had more time for each other and enjoyed the simple things in life.

NEW CHAPTER

Lucy got the keys and we went together to see our new apartment in Sydney. It was love at first sight for us both. Situated in a quiet street not far from the city centre in the suburbs, it was furnished and very clean. The furniture was mostly antique, wooden and simple. We decided to move in on the twenty eighth and our jobs started on the thirtieth. This was a new chapter in our lives and we were both very positive about it. Sometimes things feel too good to be true and this was one of them.

"Look out of the window Katie, there's a beautiful park." I went to the front room window and was greeted by the greenery of the park.

"We can watch the seasons go by here

Lucy and have some picnic time right there in the park. How about having a picnic now in the park before going back?"

"Great idea!" We went to the local deli and bought some burritos, a salad and some wine. The park was perfect for a picnic and we enjoyed relaxing in the sun surrounded by nature.

After the picnic we headed home, went to the farm, thanked everybody and collected our last pay. The next day, we packed our suitcases and Dad and Mum drove us to Sydney. They were impressed with our new apartment and we enjoyed our first meal together with them in the apartment. They stayed the night in our spare room and on Sunday they left in the morning. I was feeling nervous about the new job and hoped it would go well.

On Monday, I arrived just before nine and was met by my friend Jane in the lobby.

"Welcome to Botlex Katie, we've made a schedule for you and would like to go through that first. You'll be in the international sales department tomorrow learning from the team and Mr Fuchino wants to see you at eleven today."

"Sounds good to me Jane, I'm so pleased to be here and thank you for your recommendation, I wouldn't of got this without your help."

"My pleasure. I like to help good people and we need good people, it's a win-win." We went to her office and she showed me the schedule.

"Mr Fuchino will meet you at eleven and give you a run down on what you'll be doing. In a nutshell, you will be selling Botox which is used in cosmetic surgery and other medical uses. You will be selling internationally and meeting all sorts of people around the world in the medical industry. This business is booming and you should be able to make good commission. Let me show you around the building and help you get your bearings. After that we might just have time for a quick coffee."

We went around and I was shown how

to use the printer, where to clock in and out and where to make coffee. I met a few people but very briefly. Soon it was time to meet Mr Fuchino and Jane took me to his office.

"Welcome Katie, please have a seat. I'd like to tell you a little about the company and what you will be doing. Umm, first we were established in two thousand and eight, so that makes us a fairly new company. We are growing fast and we now employ about forty people. You will be doing international sales of Botox. First, you will learn all about Botox and practice selling it in your training. Then all going well, in about four weeks you will be our new sales representative. Are you ready?"

"I have a lot to learn, but I'm keen to start. I feel this position is good for me and I will do my very best."

"That's jolly good to hear and if you have any troubles or questions you can ask me anytime. Now, I'd like to take you to your new office. You will be working with Ms Smart and she will start your training after lunch."

"Excellent. Thank you for your time Mr Fuchino." Together we went to my new office and Ms Smart was waiting of me.

"Good morning Ms Smart. I'm all yours."

"Please call me Fiona and good morning to you. Right, first things first, here is your contract. I'd like you to read it and we will talk again after that."

"Thank you Fiona and please feel free to call me Katie." She left me to read the contract and it was easy to understand. Just as I finished reading it Fiona came into the office.

"Everything okay?"

"Yes. I signed and dated it."

"Good, I'll do the same now and you will be a probationary member of my team." She signed the contract and gave me a copy.

"Now, we'll have lunch in ten minutes,

but in the meantime I'd like to explain what you will be doing in Botlex. You will be selling Botox to new and existing customers. What do you know about Botox Katie?"

"I've been reading up on it and found lots of information. It's medical name is Botulinum toxin and it's commonly known as either Botox or Dysport. It is mainly used for facial wrinkles, muscle spasticity and muscle disorders. When used for facial wrinkles it is injected into the muscle. The drug relaxes the muscle and helps to reduce wrinkles in that area. However, it is only temporary, lasting about five months and it has to be done by a professional or serious problems can occur."

"Very good. How quickly can a patient see results with facial use?"

"After about two weeks I think?"

"That is correct. We supply mainly cosmetic surgeries and some hospitals. The problem we have at the moment is competition and this is where you come in. You will have meetings with doctors and try to sell our product. Another problem is getting time with doctors as they are always so busy. We will give you an expense account and hopefully you will be doing most of your business over lunch or dinner. We will start your training after lunch."

"Great, I look forward to that."

"Let's have a quick lunch with Jane and in the afternoon we will do some studying together about Botox. Then, tomorrow morning you will practice selling Botox with me."

We had a nice Italian lunch and studied all afternoon about Botox. I found it quite easy to understand and we also practiced explaining the product.

I finished at six and went straight home hoping to meet Lucy, but she wasn't there. I sent her a message and didn't get a reply until eight. She was still working and then they wanted to go for drinks to welcome her. I had a strange feeling this might be our new lifestyle, both very busy and sometimes I would be away for a week overseas. I tried not to be negative about it, but I started to worry about our future relationship. Could we get enough time together? Would this new lifestyle push us apart?

I decided not worry too much, but instead concentrate on my job and enjoy any time we got together as much as possible. Finally, Lucy came home at eleven, she'd had a good day and said the work looked challenging. She would eventually be in charge of schedules, pay, time off and people. She told me dealing with people was the hardest and they had issues every day, apparently it kept the HR department on their toes.

"We're going to be busy from now on Lucy. I'm going to be away on business trips sometimes and you will be working long hours. We have to be careful not to drift apart."

"Oh honey, nothing could do that! With all we've been through already we know life is going to be good. I'm hoping within one year we will be in a position to adopt and manage our work. Maybe, one of us could become a homemaker."

"That sounds ideal. I love you Lucy!"

"Me too Katie. What I really want is to settle down with you and make a family, I've had enough madness to last me a lifetime. Let's start a new chapter in our lives, do you think we can do it?"

"Lucy, we can do anything if we try."

That night I dreamed of our family life. I was the homemaker looking after three little children who were angelic. Lucy was working hard, but made time for us on the weekends and holidays. She was less wild and in my dream everything was peachy.

In accordance with the U.S.Copyright Act of 1976, the scanning, uploading, and electronic sharing of any part of this book without the permission of the publisher constitutes unlawful piracy and theft of the author's intellectual property. If you would like to use material from the book (other than for review purposes), prior written permission must be obtained by contacting the publisher. Thank you for your support of the author's rights.

Made in the USA
Middletown, DE
13 February 2019